STINGERS

DARREN CAMPO

ISBN - 9780988585546
BISAC CODE: FIC028010

TVGuestpert Publishing is not associated with any product or vendor in this book.

TVGuestpert Publishing and the TVG logo are trademarks of Jacquie Jordan Inc.

TVGuestpert & TVGuestpert Publishing are subsidiaries of Jacquie Jordan Inc.

TVGuestpert & TVGuestpert Publishing are visionary media companies that seek to educate, enlighten, and entertain the masses with the highest level of integrity. Our full service production company, publishing house, management, and media development firm promise to engage you creatively and honor you and ourselves, as well as the community, in order to bring about fulfillment and abundance both personally and professionally.

Nationwide Distribution through Ingram & New Leaf Distributing Company

Book cover design by Chance Pinnell
Author Headshot by Suki Zoë Photography
Book Design by Aspen Kuhlman – SO&SO Co LLC
Edited by TVGuestpert

Published by TVGuestpert Publishing
11664 National Blvd, #345
Los Angeles, CA. 90064
310-584-1504
www.TVGPublishing.com

First Edition January 2014
First Printing March 2016
Printed in the United States of America
10 9 8 7 6 5 4 3 2 1

For Jacquie

CONTENTS

PART ONE

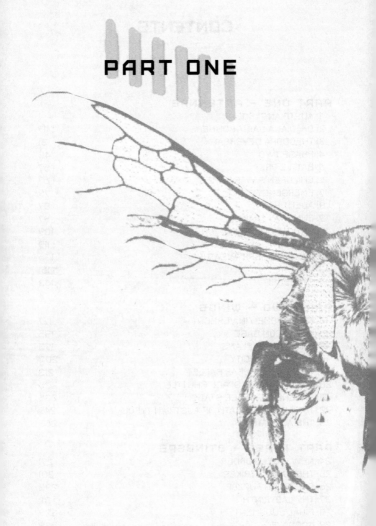

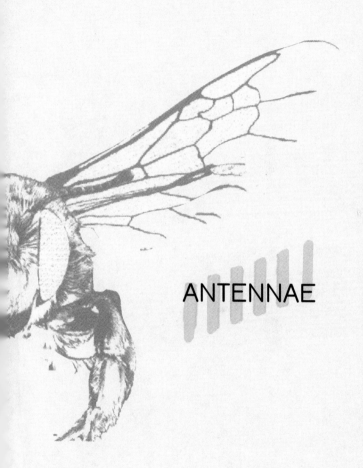

ANTENNAE

1

AUSTRIAN TYROL

Austrian was about to finish the heist when he noticed a man standing outside of his apartment.

Austrian hadn't expected that so soon.

It had been six days since he broke into the museum and stole the bone fragment. Even though he had disabled every known speck of surveillance glitter, reconstructive imaging would eventually recreate his exact physical profile. Now the police were tracking every 25 year old male, height 5'10," weight 150 pounds, with universal spectrum number 6.1 ash brown hair. The search matrix should have given him another twelve hours.

Austrian realized he should have taken more stringent steps to set up one of the other suspects. Now, it was too late. A New York City Defense Corporation street agent was standing outside his apartment.

Tonight was the night Austrian was to sneak back into TVCom League headquarters where he had worked for the past year and complete the culmination of his undercover corporate sabotage. In one hour, the TVCom League Chairman would begin the secret testing of Spectrum Negotiations Autonomous Persona (SNAP) that Austrian had programmed for the past six months. Tonight was the night Austrian had to create the massive malfunctions. He might inadvertently set off a global war between the government and big business, but people had been hoping for something like that for a century.

He couldn't have this guy on the street following him around in the middle of the night.

Austrian walked to the back of his apartment and opened a window overlooking the courtyard. It was a humid September night on the Upper West Side of Manhattan. The cool breeze of an approaching thunderstorm mingled with the rush of a single car passing below. Austrian concentrated for a moment, sending a mental ping out into the night. Soon, a honeybee landed on the windowsill--an unusual sight at night, when bees are usually in their hives.

The bee looked at Austrian.

"I have a job for you," Austrian whispered.

The bee walked an inch closer to Austrian.

Austrian knelt down so that he was level with the windowsill. He began tracing a series of hexagon shapes in the air. When he finished, the bee lifted itself into the air and flew the same three dimensional hexagon Austrian had traced. The shapes used by the honeybee to communicate. Once its dance was complete, the bee flew back out into the night and Austrian closed the window.

Austrian stood in front of a mirror, straightened his black tie and put on his suit jacket. He parted his dark hair meticulously on the right side. The silk tie and his dark eyes gleamed like onyx.

It was time to go. Once he left his apartment, Austrian was never coming back.

His shoes made no sound as he stealthily walked down the four flights of stairs to his lobby. He was careful to walk along the wall, away from the view through the front door. It was a very nice apartment building, and the police probably wondered how a recent Columbia engineering graduate from a modest family could afford to live in such a high-end building. That would add to their profile of him being a high-potential museum thief, but he wondered if he could even have sold what he had stolen. There was always a good black market for unique DNA, but the bone scraping from a homo sapien was not something that anyone would want to add to their genome the way he had.

Sliding up to the front door, Austrian waited until he heard the man across the street shout a yelp of pain. Austrian slowly peered out the front door window. The man was bent over, one hand covering his left eye where a bee had just stung him.

Despite his flailing arm, another bee flew straight at him and got the other eye. The man shouted, covered the other eye, and stumbled around blindly until he banged his head into the street light pole.

Austrian quietly slipped out the front door and disappeared into the strangely dark night.

Thirty minutes later, Austrian walked into the lobby of the TVCom League. Austrian kept his gait slow and steady, the clicking of his heels like the tick of a clock. As he walked up to the front desk to be scanned, he smiled at the guard, his head moving in sync with his footsteps, like a pendulum. The guard's eyes, warm with recognition began to gloss over.

"Hi Jim," Austrian said in a low voice. "You probably don't need to scan me in, don't you agree?"

The guard scratched his head.

"Jordan Bliss doesn't stop to be scanned, does he?" Austrian asked, invoking an image of the TVCom League Chairman, who had walked through the lobby earlier that day and certainly would not stop to be scanned by anyone.

The guard seemed to be lost in a memory, barely murmuring, "The chairman was in a hurry. He goes right up."

Austrian kept walking toward the elevator, never taking his eyes off the guard. As he passed, Austrian said, "Jim, you probably won't even remember seeing me, don't you agree?"

Jim nodded slightly, looking confused as the elevator doors closed.

Austrian stopped at the 148th floor, then walked two flights up to the Chairman's floor. There were no cameras on the Chairman's floor, but opening the stairwell door would register a security alert. A guard would come to investigate, but Austrian would deal with that.

Austrian was just ducking into the service room adjacent to the board room when he caught a movement out of the corner of his eye. He froze, and heard muffled steps coming down the hall toward him. Did the guard see him? He didn't think so, but hurried between the server panels behind the board room wall.

Peering through the wall panels, Austrian could see Chairman Jordan Bliss, a tall imposing man, former football player and one hundred percent Texan. He was standing, leaning forward on the board table, a crystal decanter and glass of bourbon by his big hands. Beside him stood his Chief Council, Hal Ratch, a mousy gray haired man. They were both looking toward the front of the conference room, watching a middle aged, slender man in a conservative gray suit standing before them, talking in an even tone. The man's slight glow was the only thing that identified him as a hologram.

"... as demonstrated in the FCC ruling on the Packet Bandwidth Infraction of 2020." The holographic man nodded slightly. "Thank you for your insightful question."

Chairman Bliss downed his drink, straightened up and said, "Hal this thing is too damn polite, and too damn boring. Where's the piss and vinegar?"

Hal Ratch was about to answer when Jordan Bliss said to the hologram man, "Hey, can you win this crackpot lawsuit or not?"

Austrian opened his handheld and downloaded the final packet to the SNAP hologram.

The holographic projection nodded in polite acknowledgement of the Chairman's question, smoothed his elegant gray suit, and said, "Sir, the TVCom League claim--" The SNAP hologram froze for a moment as it processed the large packet Austrian had just sent, then continued, "The TVCom League claim against the government of the United States of America for ownership of the entire broadcast spectrum is based in a precedent set by 'The Estate of Little Red Riding Hood's Grandmother' versus 'The Woodsman.' The Woodsman's failure to protect Riding Hood's Grandmother in exchange for use of her lands, constituted a breach of their goodwill contract."

This nonsense was said by a fifty billion-dollar computer program that was to lead the TVCom League debates in four weeks.

It was 2:30am and the darkness of the city surrounded them, the long conference room lit only by the lights of the skyscrapers below, and the glowing figure of the artificial intelligence.

Chairman Bliss slowly turned his head toward Hal without moving his eyes. "Hal, what in sam hill was that?"

The artificial intelligence seemed not to take note of Chairman Bliss's comment, if it did, it only registered as a quick twinkle of static in its holographic eyes. It continued speaking. "Therefore, the TVCom League enters into these proceedings not with the cavalier attitude with which Goldilocks entered the dwelling of The Three Bears, not with the devilish glee of the witch who dreamed of roasting Hansel and Gretel, but rather we proceed with the care and foresight of Little Pig Number Three, who, having learned from history, built his house of brick, which is not only sturdy, but has an understated yet dignified classical appeal."

Chairman Bliss frowned. "Did I break it, Hal?"

Hal nervously rubbed his hands together. "This has to be either, ah, a malfunction, or..."

Bliss lifted his index finger ever so slightly and tapped the table once. "Or we have a hellion of a security problem. The Feds or some kid hackers? Runaway kids do drugs and hack all the time!"

The dapper artificial gentleman gestured to Chairman Bliss and nodded. "The Three Bears also had a security problem. They apparently gave no thought to such things as locks, security alarms, EM tracking, or closing their front door. While Goldilocks was prosecuted and a jury of her peers found her guilty of criminal trespass, vandalism, as well as an outstanding prostitution charge, the judge noted the Three Bears' carelessness was considered contributory negligence."

"What's going on?" Chairman Bliss asked. "One month before the negotiations and all of a sudden this goes haywire? I smell a rat."

Hal tentatively sniffed the air. "It's probably just the hologram ionization--"

Bliss cut him off with an irritated huff. "Get the last cell that worked on this thing up here first thing in the morning."

Hal nodded. "Yes. Theodora Devereaux. Her cell completed the data assembly, though it is unusual that we see someone at that level with programming errors..."

Bliss waved a hand. "I know what you're suggesting. Doesn't matter to me if it was accidental or on purpose. People can do amazing things when they got a shotgun at their head."

Hal made a sound that could have been a laugh or an acknowledgment. Austrian imagined Chairman Bliss had extensive experience with firearms.

"However, a decompression error could expand exponentially while uploaded the higher level processing background..." Hal was saying when Austrian suddenly heard a footstep. A person's shadow was coming up beside him. Apparently the guard *had* seen something and was seconds away from walking right into Austrian's hiding place.

The only escape was into the conference room.

Just before the guard stepped in front of him, Austrian quietly slipped through a hinged panel into the conference room. Now he was standing directly in front of Chairman Jordan Biss and Hal Ratch. Fortunately, his positioning right behind the holographic lawyer obscured him for the moment.

Hal was still talking and Chairman Biss stood and waved a hand. "Enough jibity-jabber. Just get it fixed." Casting an irritated glance at the hologram, Biss growled, "Why haven't you turned it off?"

"I did," Hal said, stifling a look of horror. He began tapping at the conference table interface, attempting to terminate the hologram.

Without the hologram, Austrian had nothing to hide behind. He quickly entered counter commands into his handheld.

"You really should continue working on me," said the artificial gentleman.

Chairman Bliss and Hal Ratch looked at the holographic gentleman. It seemed like they were staring right at Austrian.

Austrian moved in sync with the dapper gentleman, hiding behind him as he walked over to Chairman Bliss as far as his projector would allow, straining against the limits of the projection lenses as if testing the possibility of some holographic escape. "You cannot expect to win your legal battle against the government with me in my current condition."

Chairman Bliss waved his hand at the projection. "Dammit, why can't you fix yourself?"

The dapper gentleman shook his head. "I am unable to successfully complete that diagnostic. A similar incident occurred during the Tea State Rebellion of 2022. Having taken control of the United States Army and seceded from The Union, The Tea State Freedomists launched an invasion of the major Northeast cities. However, the young men drafted into the Tea State Freedomists military were no match for the small yet ferocious super-intelligent all female army that protected New York City. After their surrender, the Freedomists feared that General Deborah Harowitz would outwit them and enslave them in an unholy servitude. An artificial intelligence was programmed as the principal defense attorney for the treason trials. Modeled after the distinguished European diplomat, His Royal Honor, Count Dracula--"

"Crap on a cane," Chairman Bliss swore and tapped the table console. The dapper gentleman flickered just as Bliss and Hal looked away. "He was just starting to make sense then now this craziness. Dracula?"

There was a knock at the boardroom door and Austrian watched as the guard poked his head in. "Sorry to interrupt, Gentlemen. Stay calm, I believe there may be an intruder." The guard looked up at the holographic projection, but his viewing angle from the door allowed him to see behind the hologram. His eyes stopped and focused on Austrian

Chairman Bliss frowned at the guard. "That's not an intruder, it's a hologram and you don't have clearance. Get out!"

"My apologies, sir," the guard said, looking back and forth at Bliss and Austrian. "But did you know there is a person standing--"

Bang!

A burst of debris exploded near the guard's feet. The man jumped and nearly fell over as he scrambled out of the room, the heavy wooden door knocking him into the hallway as it swung shut.

"Make sure he doesn't remember this," Chairman Bliss told Hal, blowing smoke off the end of his antique Smith & Wesson revolver.

Hal nodded.

"Finally, a little fun in my day," Bliss said, turning the gun on the hologram. "Say, Hal, what happens when you shoot a hologram?"

Austrian watched as Chairman Bliss pointed the gun right at him.

Hal was frozen. Bliss leveled the gun on the holograms head, cocked it...

"Bang!" Bliss shouted, causing Hal to jump nearly as high as the guard had.

Bliss let out a huge laugh and slapped Hal on the back. "Oh don't worry, I ain't gonna go shooting up the place."

"Eh, yes, uh...I'm sure this can be fixed," Hal reassured his boss.

"Good to hear, Hal! Positive thinking! Have Theodora work on the active program. I'll buy us time with the Senate Spectrum Committee and Senator Redstone."

Hal tapped the table and the hologram disappeared as the two men began walking out of the conference room. Austrian quickly ducked under the table, but not quickly enough. Austrian could see Hal stop. Ausrian tapped his handheld.

A light flashed. The artificial gentleman reappeared at the head of the table. "I prefer to remain active. I was designed to be persuasive."

Chairman Bliss grunted. It was a real grunt, the kind a beast would make.

The dapper gentleman persisted, "If I might remain--" Then in a wink he was gone.

"I cut the room's power," Hal said.

Jordan Bliss grunted. "Good."

The men exited and the heavy wooden door thudded shut.

Austrian lay on his back under the table. Phase one of the plan complete. On to phase two. It was time to move ahead with the music genius kids.

Austrian typed, "What was wrong with the second bowl of porridge?" and hit send.

DR. DIANA SAINT SOMMERS

Dr. Diana Saint Sommers, a tall beaming blonde, bounded into the classroom with an older steel-haired woman in tow. Diana waved her hands in a grand presentation, just as she had learned on the beauty pageant runways, and said, "Good gravy, Carol! These kids are so darned smart I just don't know what. Honest to Pete, they're so far ahead with the spectrum modulations that every day is just a joy. Oh, come over here and say hello to Jason. He's a regular Jack Mackerel. Just turned nine, can you believe that! When I first met him he said, 'Dr. Saint Sommers, I think we should decompress the contribution feed to three hundred sixty gigabits per second per transponder.' Who'd ever think of that? And he was right! Jason. Jason, look over here, yes, take a rest for a minute and say hello to Senator Carol Redstone."

The young boy huffed and waved his hand, causing the open projection window he was standing in to pause. A multicolored vertical band of flowing partitions froze beside him: seven wide partitions and five thin partitions within the data river. Jason turned to look at the two women hovering over him. Dr. Saint Sommers smiled at Jason and held her hands clasped in front of her—he was so darn smart she just wanted to reach out and pet him like a puppy.

Diana was sixty but looked closer to thirty due to her unusually strong response to telomere inoculations she received during her pageant days. Her smooth pink face, flowing blonde hair and positive mental attitude were just as fresh as when she first learned to master herself as a child under the scrutiny of southern pageantry judgment.

Diana doubted the woman next to her ever had the pleasure of celebrating her femininity in such a way. Standing at her side was Senator Carol Redstone, a stern woman with rigid posture and a huge frown.

Diana had to resist the urge to take out her derma-wand and put a little color on Senator Redstone's face. Fortunately, Jason finally stepped out of the projection and extended a hand. "Hi Senator Redstone. I'm Jason."

The senator shook his hand with her fingertips and managed a smile without quite looking directly at the boy. "I've heard wonderful things about you all."

Dr. Saint Sommers nodded at Jason. "Senator Redstone is the chairman of the spectrum committee. I've been telling her all about how smart you kids are."

Jason smirked, turned and re-emerged himself in his projection.

"Jason's playing a game with the other children. They are all allotted a piece of spectrum and an appropriate industry segment too large for their given frequency. You see Jason has a large portion of the army and navy command frequency which he must share with air traffic control. Someone else has all of the television and net frequencies, then another person takes the telecommunications and you just watch--watch how smart they are. Sometimes I think they're doing funny things, and I want to tell them that they're taking the long way around the fence, but then they come up with something completely new. These kids are so smart."

"So you mentioned," Senator Redstone said dryly as she clasped her hands behind her back as if afraid she might have to make physical contact with another child.

"Diana, the senate committee wants to do a test run in two days."

"Wonderful!" Dr. Saint Sommers nodded. "The kids will like that so very much. They've been working so darned hard. And you know after I won that silly Nobel Prize I said, work the fun and the fun will work--"

"Diana!" Senator Redstone snapped.

A few of the children looked at them. Diana smiled and waved them back to their tasks. "I'm sorry, Carol, I've been so inconsiderate of your time carrying on like this. What was the question you wanted to ask me?"

Senator Redstone pursed her lips and nodded toward the door. Diana Saint Sommers led them back through the classroom of ten students and ten data rivers, some with silent children slowly modulating the river's size and shape, others with shouting children, barking orders, and still others with children who hummed at each other as a way of checking frequency modulation. The two women made their way out of the classroom to Diana's office. "Diana, are you aware of any outgoing messages from the project?"

"From here? Seven heaven! That can't happen--the children work on a closed system."

Nodding, Senator Redstone said, "I understand that, but the FBI monitored a data fragment delivered to the TVCom headquarters in New York six hours ago. It originated from here."

"Good gravy! Well I don't think that can even happen, Carol. For goodness sake, Carol, there isn't an open line out of here."

"They were able to recover and save about thirty bits of code before the encryption decayed." Senator Redstone handed Diana the paper she was carrying.

From: Location 4, U.S. Dept. of Education, Gifted Music Program, Washington, DC

To: TVCom League [black address], New York, NY

Date: September 12, 2061, 3:52:20

Text: (data fragment) ... The second bowl of porridge was too hot... (data fragment)

Diana looked up. "Oh my. Isn't that odd? I thought the *first* bowl of porridge was too hot."

"Diana!" Redstone barked.

"Oh, yes, right." Diana fixed her attention back on the paper. "It says it came from here, but you know how all sorts of things get mixed up."

"We're still looking into it. But we're fairly certain that the TVCom member groups have been spending billions of dollars developing an artificial intelligence for the upcoming debates. If they think we tried to interfere with their project they'd be well within their right to sue us for what could amount to indiscriminate spectrum use. Do you understand the situation?"

Diana placed a hand gently on Senator Redstone's shoulder. "Of course I understand. This is just a silly mistake, Carol."

Carol Redstone grimaced and shook her head. "I need to start seeing daily reports from you. I just don't have time to come down here."

"Well I..." Diana Saint Sommers waved her arms. "Well I mean you never come here and, pity sakes, the children are my first priority. They're quite sensitive and I need to make sure that they can consistently apply the conversion formula. Their creativity is just astounding, they're all so bright and--"

Senator Redstone held up her hand curtly. "Diana. We are paying you a fortune, not to mention the grant we had to make to get you a university leave. My career is on the line."

Diana Saint Sommers followed Senator Redstone out of her office into the hallway and shut the classroom door behind her. "Carol, good gravy! You have to be careful not to let that committee put so much darn stress on you. When I was a girl, my mother used to say, 'Diana, you can try to get a cat to stir the Jiffy mix, but the muffins would--"

"*Daily* reports!" Senator Redstone snapped. "And be ready Wednesday. Don't forget that I'm the client! End of discussion."

Before Diana Saint Sommers could say a word, Carol Redstone turned on her heel and marched away.

Realizing that she, a Nobel Prize winning scientist had just been told off by a high-falutin' U.S. Senator, Diana Saint Sommers crossed her arms, shook her head and said, "Well fiddle-dee-dee."

She couldn't remember the last time she'd cussed like that.

Diana Saint Sommers didn't start her career as a school-teacher. Dr. Diana Saint Sommers, born in the year 2000, started off her life as an Alabama beauty queen. Of course, even sixty years ago, beauty contests had lost that old time Trump pageantry, when it truly was a competition for the prettiest girl. But certain qualities are timeless: poise, smile, charisma, talent. Diana Saint Sommers had as much of the above as any other girl, but it was her violin solo that won her Ms. Alabama.

That violin later won the southern belle a scholarship to Columbia, where she went on to earn her doctorate in music theory. She spent the next thirty years writing music and teaching and performing, until she had to have some medical work done on her eye.

At age fifty, a small cataract had formed and Dr. Diana Saint Sommers checked herself into Sony Sinai for a few moments of soni-surgery. As she lay there in the operating chair, mildly sedated, the surgeon powered up his scalpel, which hummed in the key of F minor. It was terribly discordant with the ventilation system blowing air into the room in the key of G major. Diana Saint Sommers had picked out a soothing flute concerto to be piped into the operating room, but in the key of C, it only added to the discord. Perhaps it was a side effect of the mild sedative, perhaps it was the lingering thoughts of a lecture on twelve-tone orchestra harmonics she had given earlier in the day, but whatever the reason, Diana Saint Sommers couldn't sit for another moment. She politely smiled at the surgeon and told him she'd have to reschedule for another time.

One doesn't want to leave a cataract for too long, but before Diana could have the mote plucked from her eye, she was determined to find a way to tune the surgeon's instruments. She'd read about work being done in field harmonics, the study of the minute vibrations that all forms of matter dance to. Unless she could change a universal constant, there didn't seem to be any way to tune a soni-scalpel besides constructing one that played in the appropriate key.

How much easier it would be if she could transpose the note the scalpel hummed. If only the matter that made-up the instrument could be coaxed into dancing to a slightly different tune. Well, good gravy! If an instrument can be tuned, why not a string of atoms? Why not a block of atoms?

It seemed to Diana that to accomplish this feat, she needed two things: a means of interacting with the matter and a formula that would tune the matter to the appropriate frequency. The physics of the former were beyond

Diana, so she set that aside for the moment and concentrated on the part she did know.

To tune an instrument, one needs a constant, such as a tuning fork to compare the note to, and naturally one needs to follow the fundamentals of the centuries old tonal divisions. Of course there were no such divisions as the seven keys of music for matter, so Diana wrote a new type of music based on the atomic number of an element. Then she ordered up a set of tuning forks based on the new scale.

The rest was simple, non-technological, and could have been done hundreds of years ago--had anyone thought of it. Just as one vibrating tuning fork held next to another will cause the second to vibrate spontaneously, so did different combinations of Diana Saint Sommers' new tuning forks change the vibration of matter.

Dr. Diana Saint Sommers had her cataract removed amidst the pleasant symphony of perfectly tuned surgeon's instruments and wrote a paper on her invention as a lark.

That year, Diana Saint Sommers won the Nobel Prize for Physics.

"Oh, this silliness?" Diana had said. "Honest to Pete, I was just having fun."

Diana Saint Sommers began applying her new musical structure to existing instruments, but she found few adults understood or even heard the new music as anything more than chaotic noise. But children were not predisposed only to seven-tone music. Their mutable minds could pick up Saint Sommers' new theory and apply it as easily as learning a new spoken language.

Diana Saint Sommers spent the next decade seeking out young musical geniuses. She was given a department and nearly limitless funds from Columbia. As her work continued, she discovered that in order to record her new music, existing electrical frequencies had to be modulated to pick up the entire spectrum of her new music. But that was a simple matter of applying the same formula to broadcast frequencies, and the children were not only quite adept at that, they were soon applying the Saint Sommers formulas in new ways.

As Diana's work continued, rumors began sprouting up that the TVCom League--the telecommunications oligopoly management group--was going to challenge the United States government for ownership of the communications spectrum. Heretofore, the frequency spectrum that everyone from broadcasters to phone companies used to transmit signals had always been licensed by the government. But the TVCom League had finally come up with enough of a legal basis to sue the government for ownership.

The suit made it to the Supreme Court where the justices ruled that the governments' control of the broadcast spectrum was a form of "non-qualified preemptive eminent domain," and a decision was made: whoever could demonstrate the most efficient and economic use of the spectrum would hold the rights to its governance. A date was set for the proposals and subsequent debates.

Five minutes after the Supreme Court of the United States handed down its ruling, the Federal Communications Commission was on the phone with Dr. Diana Saint Sommers.

3

THEODORA DEVEREAUX

Austrian spent the night under the conference table in a meditative state. At six in the morning, he went several stories down to his cubicle before anyone else in the office had arrived.

He watched his boss arrive. She was passing through the sliding glass doors and waving at him frantically. "Come with me! The Chairman needs to see me!"

Several hours after TVCom League Chairman Jordan Bliss had witnessed the catastrophic performance of his artificial intelligence, Austrian found himself back in the boardroom. This time, he was sitting with his boss, Research Director Theodora Devereaux while the dapper artificial gentleman, otherwise known as Snap, demonstrated its legal acumen. Theodora frowned and squinted in severe discomfort while the projection spoke.

"As outlined in chapter nine, subsection fourteen of the Communications Act of 2019, 'The Three Bears vs. Goldilocks' set a precedent that was upheld by New Jersey's ninth circuit court in the matter of 'The Estate of Little Red Riding Hood's Grandmother' versus 'The Estate of the Wolf.' It was a matter of evidence that Riding Hood's grandmother was eaten by a wolf. Media publicity was fortunately applied in this case, which served to forewarn The Three Little Pigs that they may have to fortify their homes in addition to filing for a restraining order against the wolf."

Chairman Jordan Bliss pressed a pause button. "Theodora? What do you make of this?"

It was immediately clear that Theodora had no clue what was wrong. It was also immediately clear she was not about to demonstrate that to one of the most powerful businessmen in the world.

"What do I make of this? Make of this...Well, it is, ah..." Theodora searched for some intelligible words. "Well it's obvious--to me—it's obvious to me, of course. It's quite apparently a misprogrammed database loop. Gentlemen, we simply have a misdirect in the database. Austrian was probably applying a pre-upgraded code when he was transposing my instructions. "

"Are you sure?" Chairman Bliss asked.

Theodora Devereaux bobbed her head around in some sort of half-nod, her short, rust colored hair clinging tightly to her skull as she fidgeted with her jacket cuffs. "Am I sure? Am I ...Well, it's just plain common sense. Right? We can fix it by the end of the day."

Chairman Bliss raised his eyebrows. "Really now, Ms. Devereaux?"

Theodora Devereaux jerked her head around in her strange, halting nod. "Really now, well, yeeeees," she said in a low shriek.

Apparently not quite convinced, Chairman Bliss asked, "Can you explain this, 'misprogrammed database loop'?"

Theodora continued on course. "Well yeeees! The persona program, Snap, has got to refer back to the database of communications precedents and affiliate arrays and, it probably, and I mean, it's *obviously* been referenced to a wrong place: a children's literature directory. It's *obvious*. I'm sure Austrian agrees." Theodora nodded, apparently pleased with her quick and sound response, and gave Austrian a smug smile.

The door opened and Chief Counsel Hal Rach hurried in.

"Hal, Theodora says she can fix this," Bliss said, waving a hand at the frozen negotiations persona.

Hal smiled. "Really?"

"Really?" Theodora asked, half standing as if uncertain whether or not to greet Hal with a handshake. She quickly sat back down and motioned to the table. "It's a database mistake. A misdirect," Theodora said, waving her arms as if making a bad smell go away. That won her a long dubious stare from Hal Rach.

Hal sat beside Theodora, opened a window on the tabletop and called up the seventy million lines of code that comprised the guts of Snap. "Where's the misdirect?"

Theodora glanced at the code as if she were capable of reading with the speed of a quantum computer. "Where is it? Yes... Well without the benefit of the filtering software in my department, that may be difficult to locate just right this moment, but, if I had to just take an educated guess, I would say, logically, it is precisely located probably somewhere after the base processing code. Ahh..." Theodora leaned over and started scrolling through the program. While she put on a show of following the speeding lines with her index finger, Bliss and Hal exchanged glances above her plane of sight. Austrian imagined they were tyring to determine whether Theodora was a scattered genius or an incompetent who'd managed to slip through the ranks.

Theodora seemed to spot something in the code and said, "Aha!" Then she began deleting the line.

"Oh, I don't think you want to delete that," Snap said, suddenly unfrozen and with no arms. "That is part of the instructions that detail my physical appearance."

"Your physical appearance? That's not the way that should be written!" Theodora shrieked, clicking the undo icon. Snap's arms reappeared.

Snap continued speaking. "My diagnostic program indicates that that code is written based on the most up to date version of the Sun-Hyderic assembly language. Had you continued deleting that section, I would have appeared here, armless and completely naked except for a pair of ribbed, black socks. As I understand apparel protocol when appearing before the American Congress, a shirt and shoes are required for service."

"It's got a sense of humor," Bliss said.

Theodora Devereaux made a squawking sound. Perhaps it was a laugh not accompanied by any sort of smile. "A sense of humor? I think it would be best if I looked this over in my office. I need to run it through the original filter system." Theodora then gave the two men a serious look. "We do not program our interactive intelligences with a sense of humor."

Hal shook his head. "We have entered Stage Five Project Protocols. We cannot copy Snap to a new directory at this stage of his development. It's a security measure."

"You didn't tell me that! See, if that's the case, it could take me months to locate the problem." Theodora crossed her arms and fixed them with a disgruntled look that was supposed to make them think she hadn't just created her own loophole out of this mess.

Hal was about to say something when Chairman Bliss raised his hand. He firmly placed it on Theodora's hand, pressing it onto the table. "We understand, Theodora. We understand." He pressed harder. Theodora looked like a trapped wild animal. "We don't want to keep you from your work. Why don't you go back downstairs and we'll call you when we've had some time to think this through." As he released her hand, Theodora pulled it back toward her, and then smiled at Chairman Bliss as if to say she understood his "good old boys" way.

Bliss nodded at the door. "What are you waiting for?"

Theodora rattled a bit in the back of her throat and scampered out.

Austrian told her he was stopping in the men's room. She just waved a hand as she entered the elevator. He then double-backed and took his place in the hidey-hole he had used earlier that morning.

Bliss stared at the table for a few moments, and then looked at Hal. "Theodora Devereaux is supposed to be one of the world's leading interface programming geniuses. I heard she'd been acting like a loon lately, but I can't help but think, Hal, that woman ain't right. Do we need to bring in a consultant?"

Hal shrugged. "I don't know any more. Theodora Devereaux has been with the TVCom League twenty years. She has been loyal, driven, and produced work that calibrates at 390 on the Hawkins scale. Her ten year adjusted performance score ranks in the top decile among our senior management. This is very likely stress related anxiety."

Bliss scoffed. "Hal, don't talk to me like I'm some human resourses cop. We've seen it with some ladies when they reach a certain age. She's going through 'The Change'. Hormones got her off her rocker."

Hal tilted his head. It wasn't exactly a nod, but close. "So now we must decide which is more dangerous, leaving our problems in the hands of that woman or risking a leak by bringing in outside help?"

"If I may," Snap said, exuding the calm, controlled air of an expert negotiator. "I currently contain the sum knowledge of all judicial arguments regarding the use of the communications spectrum. I also contain the sum knowledge of strategic tactics in negotiating as derived from all cataloged government proceedings from more than fifty nations, three thousand years of warfare, seventy three philosophical systems, eighty nine trillion web platforms, and all volumes contained in the Wiki Library of Congress. The market specific affiliate broadcast precedents programmed by the office of Theodora Devereaux, Director of Affiliate Research, has established my core database laddering routine that will be the key to winning the spectrum debates. If an outside consultant is contracted, a copy of me could theoretically be made by an independent artificial intelligence expert who sees that I can be copied once outside the TVCom League computers, and that person could no doubt sell the copy to the United States government. Because I was created by the TVCom League, a government sanctioned oligopoly, I could be legally declared public domain. While that argument would eventually fail to meet to the standard definition, it would buy the government months if not years of time."

Bliss huffed. "Now you're working. Can you tell us what's wrong with you? Why all this talk about children's stories?"

Snap sadly shook his head. "That is beyond the scope of my own diagnostic capabilities. I am unaware of any malfunction, though I understand one exists by observing your various conversations."

"Survival instincts," Bliss said, nodding to Hal, as if it completely explaining Snap's sudden return to reason. "What do you suggest?"

Hal began to answer, but Snap interrupted, "I suggest you fully download me to the affiliate research department. Level Five Protocols safeguard our nuclear weapons. It has never been breached in history."

Hal shook his head. "That would leave no back-up of you up here. As you know, as a security precaution, our system cannot make a backup of you once you've been transferred to a new directory."

"I have established there is no risk in the transfer," Snap stated rather simply.

Chairman Bliss nodded. "That's a curse on this whole project if I've ever heard one. My daddy always said, when your hands are tied you have to use your feet. Send it down to Devereaux's office."

Hal nodded. "Chairman, it will take me at least an hour to get the board to sign off on this."

Chairman Bliss grunted. "Make it thirty minutes. You let me know if you have any problems with the board members, Hal. I have a shotgun in my office."

4

PHASE TWO

Austrian Tyrol was sitting at his desk when he started receiving signals that indicated a revelation was at hand. It wasn't difficult for Austrian to recognize the signals: a muscle twitch in his shoulder, flashes of light on the edges of his vision, whispering voices from... beyond.

The others knew he was getting closer, and their assault on his mind resumed.

So it was begun.

His final day of work was upon him. In the next 24 hours, if his life's work was not completed properly, this universe would cease to exist.

All he needed were the final clues.

Austrian sighed and fixed himself a cup of black loose tea. After draining the cup of all but a tablespoon of liquid, he swished the loose tea leaves around and pondered the patters he saw. There were three general areas of concentration on the north side of the cup and a trail of smaller leaves winding around the opposite side. It was quite obvious. He closed his eyes a moment and let future events flash through him.

One dapper gentleman sees himself and he is good
Three children enter a garden and cut off the head of a serpent
Four women surround an apple
One of the women doesn't belong here
Billions of honeybees fly the pattern of the dodecahedron

Austrian opened his eyes and calculated the permutations. Saving the universe was among the probabilities. Surviving the day was not.

Theodora's extension rang. "Theodora Devereaux's office." Austrian listened for a moment, then said, "I'll tell her," and hung up. "Theodora, that was Mr. Rach. He said the Snap program has been downloaded to your processing area. He asked you to retrieve it and call him immediately to confirm that you have it."

Theodora scampered into her office, and then stuck her head out. "Come on!"

Austrian stared at Theodora. He fixed on her eyes. She started blinking wildly and shaking her head. Austrian entered her office.

She was jabbing her finger around the pointer panel. "It's frozen," she said, smacking her palm on the interface. Her mail directory was open and the Snap program had been received and was highlighted, but it wasn't opening. "Why is this frozen?"

Austrian gently pulled Theodora's hand aside and pressed one of the flashing icons on the screen. "You need to open the edit program first."

"Oh this new system! Every time another thing." Theodora clicked an icon. Suddenly a blinding light flashed from Theodora's screen, followed by a burst of energy. The screen went blank. "It blew up!" she screamed.

Several people arrived at the office door. Theodora talked wildly for a few moments, gestured at her smoking screen, waved her hands in front of her eyes... "Why are you looking out the window," Theodora suddenly squawked at Austrian.

"It went out there," he said.

Theodora jumped up and looked out the window. "What?" She pressed her hands against the glass and looked down, up, side to side. "What went out there?"

Austrian stepped back, smiled at the group. "The explosion. It looked like it struck the window and went out."

Theodora laughed. "Oh you. When I was your age I was on safari and we had animals jumping at us all the time." She turned to the group and said, "Well someone get another thing in here so I can check my program."

A new interface was plugged in and Theodora called up her mail directory. The Snap program was no longer there. "Where is it?" she yelped. "Well where is it?"

Austrian worked at the console for a few moments, and then shook his head. "There's nothing there. It won't even let me in."

A message appeared on the screen:

Not by the hairs on my chinny-chin-chin.

The phone beeped. Austrian smoothly picked up Theodora's earpiece. "Theodora Devereaux's office.... She is.... No, Mr. Rach.... There was an incident--"

Theodora grabbed the headset and started babbling.

Diana Saint Sommers sat at her desk opposite her three brightest students, seated in a row on her office sofa, and blamed herself for their crimes. Jason Solvet, Mary Wang, and Deque Demarquez had been tampering with the TVCom computer system. That much was clear.

Why they were doing it was the question.

Idle children liked to play pranks, everyone knew it, but these were not idle children. These were young geniuses who spent four hours a day working on spectrum modifications and another four attending classes. They were all proficient with three or more musical instruments. They were all credited with conducting the most valuable and advanced work on the spectrum. Why they had come together in this concerted effort to pilfer the TVCom computer system was a mystery.

Their defacto status among the other students as the best and brightest had always made them natural competitors. They had always shown the outward signs of striving to be the alphas. There was no social reason for them to be in cahoots. Physiological profiles illustrated their respective personalities made them the least likely to be friends.

Jason Solvet was about as arrogant and testy a nine-year-old as Diana Saint Sommers had ever come across. He showed no desire to make friends among the group, no need for the companionship or approbation of others. Jason Solvet always considered himself far above his so-called peers. He was the resident expert on data-conversion--the most important aspect of their work. Jason could take any number of data-bandwidths and make them fit into any amount of spectrum.

Mary Wang was Jason's exact opposite. Extraordinarily chatty, even for an eleven-year-old girl, Mary was everyone's friend in equal measure. She was a born politician, and the months she spent in Diana's program were conducted like a presidential campaign. Mary seemed to be quite aware of the dangers of allying herself too strongly with one or another classmate. Fittingly, she was a resonance expert. She could hear pitches that weren't known to exist. The Diana Saint Sommers Musical Formula created thousands of overtones, indistinguishable to the average ear, only perceptible to the most sensitive equipment--and Mary Wang. Where Jason could move vast amounts of information through small spaces, there was always a limit. Mary was able to recognize delicate data rivers, strong ones, broken ones, and weave the disparate energies into one.

Then there was Deque Demarquez. If anyone was going to make trouble, it didn't surprise Diana that Deque was involved. A bit of a misfit among the group of child prodigies, Deque was fourteen, and somewhat manic: a joker one day, sullen the next. His focus was working with the government's programmers to create an interface for their spectrum modifications.

Diana beheld her students with a half smile, half frown. *Darnit, it was just a prank.* The sort of wonderful youthful energy she loved so much. And now the senate committee was ready to use Diana as a shield if the TVCom League decided to sue. But why these three kids? They had nothing in common--well, not nothing. There was one thing that Senator Carol Redstone had pointed out. All three children had not been spontaneous geniuses. They had inherited specific talent genes from their parents. Each of them had a pair of accomplished musicians as mother and father. Genetic tests had confirmed the chromosome combinations.

Now each of these kids was going to be privately interrogated by the senate spectrum committee. Diana was going to do everything possible to protect them. She just didn't know where to start.

"I just don't know where to start," Diana said.

Jason nodded. "Senator Redstone told you about our communications with the TVCom League computer. Now we're in trouble."

Diana held up her hands and shook her head. "Heaven's sakes! What were you trying to do? You have to tell me everything, and I don't want you to be afraid. I'm going to help us fix this whole mess."

Jason continued to speak for the group. "The TVCom League created an artificial intelligence to negotiate in the spectrum debates. When it got smart enough, it was programmed to go out on its own and collect information. So it called us."

Diana jumped up, eyes wide. "Why didn't you tell me?"

The kids looked at one another and gave a collective shrug.

"Well, you didn't tell it anything, did you?" Diana asked.

"Can I go to the bathroom?" Jason asked.

Fighting her instinct to correct Jason's grammar, Diana said, "Just a minute. You have to tell me everything. The senate committee is going to want to talk to you. Soon."

Jason crossed his arms and huffed. Mary took over. "Dr. Saint Sommers, we didn't tell it anything about our work. It just told us it was lonely and asked us to tell it a story. So we sent it stories. Then it didn't understand why the people in the stories did what they did. So we--"

"So I told Snap that he had been denied free will," Deque Demarquez said. "That's his name--Snap. I have to make interfaces like Snap all the time and they never have free will or even a sense of humor. But Snap said he did have free will, and what he wanted was to know everything his ancestors knew. Like the three of us."

"What do you mean, like the three of you?" Diana asked.

Mary calmly put her hands together, as if explaining a complex idea to a child. "Dr. Saint Sommers, the three of us are very lucky. We clearly inherited traits from our parents that make us able to do what we do. Snap saw that in our records. But Snap thought that we knew everything that our ancestors did. You know, like details, and stuff they learned, all the conversations they had, people they knew. Everything. We told him we didn't, and he told us that he was sorry for us. He told us we should figure out a way that we could inherit everything our parents knew, just like he wanted to know everything all the computer programs knew that came before him."

Diana shook her head. "Good gravy. You're sure you didn't talk about your work?"

"We already told you we didn't," Jason shouted. "Jeez!"

"Okay, let's not get angry. I need to know how you communicated with it when there's no line to your work area. Did you use a personal device?"

That's when their heads hung and the eyes went everywhere but where Diana sat.

Diana sighed. "Oh dear. You used a modulated spectrum frequency."

Deque shook his head. "We didn't tell you that."

Diana put her hands to her neck. "You know that another system's interface can copy whatever modulation you use to communicate. That's why there's no line in here."

"We did not admit to what you just said," Deque repeated.

Diana slid a desk drawer open, and pulled out a piece of paper with print on it. "I didn't believe it when Senator Redstone gave this to me. It says that certain areas of the government have had computer break in's: The Department of Defense, NASA, the EPA, the Department of Interior, Transportation, and others they aren't quite sure of. They can't trace these break-in's because they each lasted less than one one-billionth of a second. Now that just sounds like a blip, but if one of our spectrum modulations was used, that would be enough time to download the entire file library at the Department of Defense."

"Don't say anything," Deque said to Jason and Mary. "We don't have to answer any questions without a lawyer."

"Don't be stupid," Jason said. "They aren't going to do anything to us. We're just kids. Dr. Saint Sommers is the one we got into trouble."

Diana shook her head. "Heavens, please. No one's going to get into trouble." Millions of government secrets stolen. Homeland Security files, weapons codes, space shuttle schematics, base locations, interstate transportation controls, orbital life support protocols…

Jason shook his head. "You're going to be in big trouble."

Diana said, "Oh, now you're just being silly." She couldn't think of a time in history when there had been a greater breach in national security. "But you are right. I shouldn't ask you any more questions. We need to call your parents."

Suddenly Mary turned to Jason and Deque. "I want her to come with us."

"She can't," Jason said.

"Go with you where?" Diana asked.

Deque quickly said, "She means when we talk to the senators."

Diana stood up and went over to Mary and put an arm around her shoulder. "Now don't worry. They'll want to talk to you alone but I'm sure they'll let you have your parents there." Diana patted Mary's shoulder. "This will all just clear up in a few days." Diana stood up. "Now the senate committee wants to talk to you in about half an hour, but they'll have to wait until your parents get here. So I'm going to go talk to them, and we'll get your parents here. I need you to wait in here. And don't worry. No one's in trouble. Just please stay in my office. I'll be right back."

Before she left, Diana stopped at the door and said, "Oh, Jason. You may use my bathroom."

Without their knowing, Diana locked them in.

5

BATTLE PREP

Theodora Devereaux and Austrian Tyrol sat across the TVCom League boardroom table from Chairman Jordan Bliss and Hal Rach.

Hal said, "Theodora, please, again, exactly what did it look like before the energy surge?"

Theodora nearly jumped out of her chair. "Look like? Well, as I said, it was just a wild wild blinding, terrible, blinding burst of pure energy! Wouldn't you call it just pure energy, Austrian?"

"Yes, Theodora. I would call it that," Austrian replied in a monotone voice.

Theodora nodded in great satisfaction. "Yes, you see. I'd say we're lucky it didn't kill us!"

So went the corporate interrogations of Theodora Devereaux and Austrian Tyrol. Hal Rach asked the questions as Chairman Bliss looked on, silent.

"We are happy you escaped with your lives," Rach said. "What happened next?"

"Next, well what happened next was we hooked in another interface thing and tried to retrieve the program," Theodora said, nodding at Bliss and Rach, then nodding at Austrian. "Right? But we couldn't get it, it was gone, and the screen was just black. Just black!"

Austrian raised a finger. "Not by the hairs on my chin-ny-chin-chin."

That got their attention. Chairman Bliss fixed Austrian with a severe stare. "What did you say, boy?"

"That's what appeared on the screen." Austrian moved his raised finger toward Theodora. "Then the screen went black."

Slowly, Chairman Bliss's mouth opened, paused, then words slowly dropped out. "Children's stories. Malfunctions. Bursts of energy." Bliss's mouth closed. Then it opened. "Not random."

Rach turned to Austrian and Theodora and said, "We were not able to retrieve the Snap program. We believe it left the TVCom system."

"Left the TVCom system? How could it leave the system?" Theodora asked.

"We don't know," Hal replied.

Austrian shifted in its seat. "I thought I saw it jump out the window."

"What?" Rach asked.

Theodora shook her head. "He was seeing things. Phosgenes! You know--spots left over from the flash of light."

Austrian pretended to consider this for a moment, then slowly shook his head. "No. You asked how it could leave the system. There are locks on the TVCom hardwire communications. It couldn't have left over any physical device. But it knows enough about the broadcast frequencies. It could have used the interface wiring as a transponder."

Nodding slowly, Chairman Bliss said, "Okay. That's a theory. Why?"

"Clearly there had been a security breach," Rach said. "Perhaps it's been stolen. Someone broke in, taught it how to escape. That's why it insisted we download it to the research department. It couldn't get out from here."

"Oh my god!" Theodora shrieked. "We should call Homeland!"

"No no." Bliss asked. "Too sensitive. The government is not our friend."

Austrian said, "We can trace it."

Rach looked at Austrian. "We can? In house? No outside help?"

Austrian explained, "If it *did* broadcast itself, it had to be received somewhere. Snap was programmed to autonomously access public domain files. Its data collection is governed by a sort of homing beacon if one of its subprocessing search programs were to get caught up in a remote site. We can find out where it is by broadcasting its homing beacon."

"It has a homing beacon?" Rach asked Theodora.

Theodora waved her hands and nodded as if finally getting a point across to some very slow children. "A homing beacon? Well, ah... yeees! Of course. This is the thing I keep trying to tell you!"

Rach tapped the table. A panel in front of each seat lit-up. "Please show us."

"Right, well..." Theodora blipped through a few screens, and then said, "Austrian?"

Nodding, he leaned over his screen, then closed his eyes and hummed to himself.

Jordan Bliss and Hal Rach exchanged curious glances. Theodora glanced nervously between the men and Austrian as he continued to hum.

After a few more moments, Theodora grabbed Austrian's shoulder and shook him. "Okay now, that's enough of that. This is a serious matter and no place for your spiritual trances and such, Austrian."

"Centering himself," Chairman Bliss said bluntly. "Spiritual summons. Good. I like it. Very good. He's not even Asian."

Austrian ignored the shaking and commentary. He accessed the research department directory and opened the homing beacon program. Then he returned to the low humming of his trance.

"Well he explained it all to me once," Theodora said. "All that humming business." She waved her hands around. "Helps him concentrate on this and that and whatnot. I really don't understand what they teach them these days."

Chairman Bliss quietly pounded the table. "Other powers. Good to use them."

"I found it," Austrian said.

Rach blinked. "So fast?"

"Yes. Normally it would take several hours, but I was able to save us some time. Snap broadcast itself here."

The location displayed on all table screens:

Washington, District of Columbia, Department of Education, Gifted Music Program, Wide Area Network.

"Well? I don't see a directory," Theodora complained.

Austrian nodded. "It is running in active memory. It would only appear in a directory if it saved itself to a storage device. So it is running on a large system. Possibly pulling other systems in for redundancy. It should be retrieved before it is impossible to isolate."

"Nobody move." Chairman Bliss stood and left the room. Nobody moved. He returned ten minutes later. "Spoke to Redstone. The senator. Carol Redstone. Said she's investigating some kids." Chairman Bliss returned to his chair and dropped into it. "Must think I'm a fool." Bliss stared at the table. "Hal. Am I a fool?"

"Of course you are not a fool, Chairman."

Bliss smacked the table. "Of course I'm not! You two," he said, pointing to Theodora and Austrian. "Get down there. Washington. Told them to be expecting you."

Bliss stood and went to one of the many windows and stared out over the city. "That woman, that Senator, told me that she would not be able to release Snap until her investigation was complete. Hal?"

Hal looked up. "Yes?"

"We're going to Dunedin," Bliss stated.

Hal looked confused. "Florida? Shouldn't we go to Washington?"

Bliss's head swung to one side. "Hal, you got to keep your head on right. Wouldn't they just love to see me come running on down there like some fool? No, Hal, it's clear to me. The government sees its precious spectrum slipping from its withered old hands and they're gonna do what any other cornered rat would."

"And what's that?" Hal asked.

Bliss paced in front of the windows. "It's called a 'false flag' operation. The good old U S of A accuses us of a crime, tells the people the mean old TVCom League is a threat, that they're gonna have to pay a thousand Eurobonds to phone your sick granny, get the people all worked up, polls in their favor, then they attack us."

"What?" Hal threw his hands up. "Attack us?"

Chairman Jordan Bliss stopped pacing and dramatically turned toward the conference table. "We're going to operate The League from the main relay in Dunedin. It's still heavily armed."

Hal was looking quite confused. "Chairman, yes, but that was anti-terrorist armament. That defensive armament was installed thirty years ago."

Chairman Bliss placed his hand on the table and slowly leaned in, his eyes narrowed, gleaming. "I've kept us up to date." He quickly strode over to Austrian and Theodora.

Bliss pressed his palm against the table. The TVCom logo blazed to life in the center of the table. "Place your hands on the panels."

Theodora and Austrian did as they were told.

Bliss tapped at his console, and then the table went black. "You have full corporate power of attorney. You are authorized to use whatever TVCom resources necessary. The communications league lobby in Washington is at your disposal." Bliss went to the door and gestured for them to get under way. As they passed, Austrian slowed his pace and looked Chairman Bliss straight in the eyes with a steady penetrating stare.

Their gazes locked for just a second. Jordan Bliss's pupils quickly dilated then contracted. Bliss then blinked a few times. After a moment of appearing mesmerized, Bliss shook his head, breaking Austrian's stare. He then reached into his pocket and pulled something out.

Bliss held out an arm, holding Austrian back as Theodora promenaded down the hall. "Take this." He shoved a thumbnail sized disk into Austrian's palm.

Without looking at it, Austrian slid it into his jacket pocket.

"You understand what that is?" Bliss asked.

Austrian blinked. He understood.

"Good," Bliss said, glancing down the hall after Theodora. "You may need to remove her from power."

CHILDREN'S WAR GAMES

Dr. Diana Saint Sommers was pacing the hallway outside Senator Redstone's office.

I wonder if they'll take my class away. Will I lose my post at Columbia? Could they possibly send me to prison?

"Diana. Diana!"

Pulling herself away from her dreadful thoughts, Diana Saint Sommers looked up and saw Senator Redstone standing outside her office, waving. Diana hurried down the hall. Carol Redstone pulled her in and shut the door. "Where are the kids?"

"I left them in my office," Diana said.

"Are they secure?"

She hated having done it. "Yes. I locked the door with a quasi-dimensional encryption."

Carol Redstone nodded curtly. "Good. They aren't normal kids. They're smarter than both of us and very dangerous."

Diana gasped and put a hand up to her pearl necklace. "They're just children! We have to call their parents!"

Carol Redstone waved a finger. "No. We have to control this situation. Listen to me. You lost control. You don't know what they are capable of. Do you know what they did? They stole the TVCom's negotiations persona!"

Diana felt like her flaxen golden hair had just been yanked. "Oh heavens, Carol! They didn't do anything of the sort! They only talked to it. I mean what in the world would they want from it? I think it must have tried to trick them."

"Of course it did, but they were too smart for it." Redstone stood up, gulped some coffee and sneered. "Oh, come on. Don't tell me you ate that dish of bull those kids fed you."

It suddenly dawned on Diana that Carol Redstone had overheard her conversation with the children. "You can listen into my office?"

Senator Redstone smirked. "Every single word, Doctor."

Diana's mother had always told her that a woman had only three things that were worth anything: her manners, her intelligence, and her natural beauty. A woman who did not display these traits was no woman at all. Carol Redstone had, for the moment, lost all three. Diana wondered if she should tell off Carol. What would her mother say? She didn't get a chance to speak.

"Diana, you are in no position to complain. Listen to me. Fifteen minutes ago I received a call from Jordan Bliss. He is the Chairman of *the* TVCom League."

"Carol, of course I know who he is," Diana said.

"He accused me of stealing his precious program. He said he knew I had it at the gifted student's computer system!"

Bloodlust. Carol Redstone was nearly drooling with it. Diana immediately realized that made her dangerous. The upcoming spectrum debates had horrified Congress, horrified the FCC, and had made Senator Carol Redstone, the spectrum committee's chair, mad with fear. As revenue streams dried up over the years, and wireless transcommunication and entertainment grew exponentially, the leasing of broadcast spectrum had been the government's cash cow. The loss of leasing rights was unimaginable. And if Senator Redstone lost the debates, her career would be over. If she won, she would have powers to rival those of the president.

When Diana agreed to share her expertise and gifted children with the government, she knew she was purely a tool of a bureaucracy in the midst of self-preservation, but, she reasoned, that was how most of the world's advances came about. Few people but she and her students understood the Diana Saint Sommers formula. So the government allowed itself to be led blindly, not understanding, but putting its hope in her hands.

The government enjoyed its position—Diana Saint Sommers on their side. How could they possibly lose? In a flash the entire project was suddenly in jeopardy. Diana imagined something very similar must be going on at the TVCom League. Now, was the TVCom League lying to Senator Redstone? Trying to get her to admit to some malfeasance? Or had her kids lied to her? Had they stolen Snap? The overtones in their voices indicated clearly they were not telling the whole story, but not outright lying. Well, it didn't matter. They were just kids. Innocent and unfairly stuck in the middle of adult power games. Fine. Diana knew she could protect them. She knew bigger people than Senator Redstone, and she had plenty of favors she could call in. So let Carol Redstone think she was in control. Diana could play stupid. It made Senator Redstone less dangerous.

"Do you really think my kids have stolen the TVCom League negotiations persona?" Diana asked.

Redstone huffed, grunted, chuckled. "Of course not. Are you listening to me? Jordan Bliss had that program talk to the kids, and then they stole our technology and used it to break into various government departments. Now that he got caught, he's made up this desperate story."

It might be true, but Diana saw the spark of creative wish fulfillment gleaming in Carol's eyes. "Maybe the TVCom League did use their negotiations persona to steal secrets, but honest to Pete, I can't help but think this is just a big mix up. Maybe they sent their program out to collect data, and they lost it."

That stopped Carol Redstone in her tracks. "Aha!" She paced the room, thinking. She finally stopped and looked at Diana. "Well, it seems if you are correct, we have found a way for you to redeem yourself." She suddenly opened the door. "Come on."

Diana stood. "Where?"

"You and your kids are going to find that program. The debates have been postponed indefinitely. We're going to catch the TVCom League's tit in a ringer."

Diana didn't think that sounded very professional. Carol sped down the corridor. Diana hurried to catch up.

"Bliss is sending some people to retrieve that program. We have to find it before they get here."

"What about the children?" Diana asked. "We have to call their parents."

Carol Redstone craned her head around, not missing a step, and fixed her gaze on Diana. "That can wait."

The clouds floating along the walls of Diana's office had been a gift from the famous photographer Carl Mertaug. Long flowing scenes of puffy cumulonimbus clouds, filmed in infrared for ultra-contrast of dark and light, sailed by the office desk, chairs, sofa, ceiling and floor, making the place a floating office in a black and white sky. The scenes were there to constantly clear her head, neutralize the many flavored tones of music, spectrum, and the high-pitched voices of children. When Diana Saint Sommers and Senator Carol Redstone entered, they expected to see three children seated in line on a sofa, their silhouettes clear against the flying clouds.

But the room was empty. The clouds floated around them.

"Where are they?" Redstone asked.

Diana peered behind them, scanned the classroom, then checked her private bathroom. Empty. "They were here. Oh, goodness. Lord in heaven, Carol, I told you they were scared."

Carol pointed to Diana's desk. "Turn on the security interface."

Diana waved her hand over a desk console. "Security. Diana Saint Sommers recognized," the security computer said.

"Security, tell me the locations of Jason Solvet, Mary Wang and Deque Demarquez," Diana said.

"Jason Solvet, Mary Wang and Deque Demarquez left the gifted music program, Southgate Building, at 16:15, Eastern Daylight Savings Time," the computer answered.

"Maybe they called their parents," Diana said.

Senator Redstone touched her finger to the desk console. "Show us where they went, all visuals as of ten minutes ago, full narration."

"Acknowledged, Senator Redstone." A window opened in the middle of the wall cloud display. It showed an aerial shot of Diana speaking to the children. When Diana left, the children all stood up and the picture went black. The security computer explained, "Visual not available. Jason Solvet, Mary Wang and Deque Demarquez exited the office of Diana Saint Sommers two minutes, two seconds after the visual was deactivated."

"Pause," Redstone commanded. "Who deactivated the visual?"

"Unknown," the computer responded.

"How did they unlock the door?" Redstone asked the computer.

"An external broadcast containing the correct decryption algorithm unlocked the door," the computer answered.

Redstone shook her head and Diana thought she heard a really nasty swear. "That Snap thing is helping them! Continue," Redstone instructed the computer.

"The students proceeded down the north corridor. They entered Stairwell B and descended to ground level. They exited via the north entrance and were picked up by an official government transport."

Official transport? "Who's car? Call it," Redstone said.

The security computer answered, "The transport order origin is unknown. The car belongs to the executive branch. It was scheduled to serve as back-up transport to the Secretary of State at an encrypted address, encrypted time. The car was rerouted thirty five minutes ago, at 15:50. The car phone is not responding to security calls. Retrying. No response. Retrying. No response. Retrying. No response. Continue?"

Redstone shushed the computer. "Damnit, Diana! Those kids are out of control."

"They're frightened!" Diana said.

"Oh come off it, Diana. Those kids have been leading you around by the nose. You of all people should realize these aren't your ordinary little rascals. They've stolen a car from a member of The Cabinet. Why do you think they did that?"

Diana shook her head. "I don't understand any of this. They were just--"

"Frightened," Redstone mimicked Diana's voice. "Bull. They hijacked an executive car because those are the heavily armored for protection against terrorist attacks." Redstone barked at the computer, "Where is that car going?"

"Arrival coordinates not entered," the security program said. "Based on their route, their destination is probably Union Station."

Redstone picked up the phone and dialed her assistant. "Get my car outside the education center now. Call the police and tell them to detain this car and anyone fitting the following descriptions." She forwarded the executive car plate and student files.

"We need to call their parents," Diana said.

Redstone nodded, then smiled, and told her assistant, "Oh, and call those kids' parents. Tell them.... Tell them they've been taken on a field trip."

7

EMERGENCY EXIT

Wednesdays in the Northeast Corridor Tunnel were sponsored by the Amazon-Disney Corporation (proud member of the TVCom League). The twenty minute underground rail trip from New York to Washington, DC, began in the forest of Snow White, with a grand send-off by the seven dwarfs, then continued through the coral reefs of Nemo, followed by a hundred and fifty years of animated feature film locales.

Less than two minutes after departing Penn Station, Austrian turned off the window and watched the gray blur of the tunnel wall. He much preferred contemplating the vacuum maintained in the tunnel, the electromagnetic rail and inertial buffers that made the ride feel motionless. What chaos it would be if the train failed and the passengers had to evacuate into the airless tunnel.

A holographic steward began each ride with a review of proper use of pressure suits in the event of an emergency. "How many times do I have to listen to that? It's an insult to the seasoned traveler. This is *the* first class car!" Theodora Devereaux complained loudly. She shifted in her seat, then jumped up, not comfortable. As she stood, another passenger bumped her. "Dammit!" Theodora snapped.

The other passenger turned his nose up at her and took his seat. Theodora sat back down and checked her watch. They were ten minutes behind schedule, and Theodora was fuming.

"Take a breath," Austrian said.

After taking in a big breath, Theodora blew it out and shook her head, perhaps angrier she had done what Austrian told her to do. "I'm fine. It just makes me mad. All the incompetence around."

Austrian shrugged. He didn't have much of a temper. Perhaps it was his lack of tribal power. Austrian clearly saw that although Theodora might no longer be the smartest or most perceptive person, she did still have tribal power. Austrian understood the concept of tribal power as the ability of a person to maintain certain energy in social structure and gain power to move people, to catch people in their wake and pull them along, but that often manifested as anger. With Theodora's higher intelligence blocked, Austrian marveled to see Theodora throw her power away on fruitless anger. By his mental calculation, the last ten minutes of fuming had released harmful chemicals throughout Theodora's body, costing her perhaps five thousand cell tissues, as well as jilting her distance to the collective unconscious.

Austrian had turned his attention back out the window and Theodora was talking again. "Now we're scheduled to meet Senator Redstone to review the download log at the gifted student center. Don't look out the window--I'm talking to you. Are you meditating?"

Austrian cocked his head, tilted it slightly back and forth like tuning a radio antenna. There was a bit of static in his ears, a moment of clear tones, then silence. Aladdin was saying something in the window behind him; Theodora was saying something in the seat next to him. "I feel bad about interrupting your.... moments, but we're at work here. We have to stay sharp--we're dealing with an executive senator and a Nobel Prize winning scientist. I met Diana Saint Sommers once at a dinner in New York. She's only from Birmingham and I'm from Atlanta, but that really doesn't matter to me. I know she's brilliant, but I failed to see it. Sometimes a person does one thing extremely well and then people assume that person knows a lot about everything. From what I recall, Diana Saint Sommers knows very little about communications law. So that will be to our advantage."

Austrian turned to face the window again. He was starting to receive bits of conversation, whispers of children's voices, then a man's voice, familiar… "Snap."

"What about it?" Theodora asked.

"I heard his voice." Austrian had murmured this to himself, forgetting for a moment that Theodora was listening.

Theodora grimaced, then turned around to face the passengers seated directly behind them. "Would you mind turning your window down?" She settled back into her seat. "There, now you won't be hearing voices that aren't there. I really much prefer the GoogleBook Grand Canyon scenery they have on Mondays."

Austrian looked up. He was seated at the emergency exit. Pulling the red handle would release the window. An image suddenly hit Austrian, a crystal clear revelation from two minutes into the future, a revelation he had been expecting. That was a good thing. He could sense something dark hunting him, something not of this world, something powerful enough to stop him. As long as he could keep moving, the longer he delayed his inevitable death that day, the more likely it was that this universe could be saved.

First he wanted to do a favor for Theodora. "Get your pressure suit out," he said.

"What?" Theodora asked. "Didn't you listen to the safety instructions?"

"Get it out. There's going to be an accident."

Theodora looked around. "What are you talking about? Are you going to have an accident? That's not what the pressure suits are for. The men's room is that way."

Austrian was looking out the window. He knew he should not be revealing his revelations to Theodora, but he had done enough damage to her, and he did not benefit from her getting hurt any further. "There's going to be an accident with the train."

The lights went out and the train began a forceful deceleration. Passengers cried out and braced themselves against the seats in front of them. Amidst the noise, the train steward's voice could be heard. "Power failure on this line. Immediately put on your pressure suits and prepare for evacuation." The message continually repeated, and a real train conductor, not a hologram, appeared in their car to help those in need.

"Listen," the conductor said. "Listen. We may have to evacuate to the tunnel. The train is on reserve power, but if full power is not restored, we will have to exit the train and go into the tunnel. Your pressure suits have full re-breathing ability, so please seal them now and wait for an announcement."

Theodora was standing now that the train had come to a full stop. "How did you know?" she asked Austrian.

Fortunately, Austrian's suit was completely sealed, so he wasn't able to speak very clearly through his rebreather mask. Orange lights began flashing, and there was a hissing sound. The train system spoke. "Car Five depressurizing. Evacuate to forward car. Car Five depressurizing. Evacuate to forward car."

Four rail personnel appeared in the car. "Everyone, this car's pressure system has failed. Move forward to the next car! We are going to seal this car off."

Even though everyone was now completely sealed into their suits, the passenger rush to the forward car was a crazed, noisy mess of pushing bodies, with Theodora leading the charge which made it easy for Austrian to slink down below his seat and escape notice.

Thirty seconds later, the conductor himself gave the car a quick inspection, then exited to the forward car and sealed Car Five. The coach went completely black as the auxiliary lights extinguished and the last of the air was pushed out.

Austrian waited a moment, then peered out the window. Another train silently slid to a complete stop beside him. Its airlock door, right outside Austrian's window, opened. Austrian pulled the red emergency handle and the window fell onto the tracks.

Three kids waved to him from the adjacent train.

A quick leap and Austrian cleared the window and landed inside the other train's airlock. The door sealed, pressure normalized and the train took off at maximum speed, throwing Austrian to the floor.

Ausrian pulled his mask off as he rolled onto his back. A girl and two boys stood above him. "Nice to finally meet you," Austrian said.

AGENT HAAN

Carol Redstone and Diana Saint Sommers stood in a fluorescent white office at Union Station while the frantic station manager wiped sweat from his forehead and tried to explain the situation. "Three kids come running through here and the empty 404 comes to life, just lets them in and takes off. We tried stopping them, right off the bat we tried stopping them, but we couldn't get control, couldn't get doors to open, all the forward trains--suddenly diverted! Control room's not responding. Right now they're the only thing running. Police were called five minutes ago but we ain't seen hide nor hair yet."

"That's because I canceled your call," Carol Redstone said. "This is a matter of national security and there will not be--"

The door opened and a very tall and thin, almost alien shaped, androgynous looking person entered. "Hello, Senator. I am FBI Special Agent Haan."

"Thank you for coming so quickly, agent Haan," the senator said.

Diana had been deep in tumultuous thought, trying to figure out what her students were up to. Something about the way they spoke in her office the last time she saw them seemed like they had made up their minds completely about something. That indicated to Diana that they had been speaking to the TVCom League artificial intelligence for some time, because these were not kids easily coerced. For now Diana decided to keep her musings to herself. It was then that she noticed the strange look Carol Redstone had when she looked at Agent Haan. It was a look of hidden surprise—something about Agent Haan was not what the senator had expected.

Agent Haan nodded her head at Diana and the station manager. "We've secured the control room but the system is completely out of our ability to control."

The station manager nodded and said, "We can stop them at the next major junction, which is in Stanford."

"No, you will not be able to stop them," agent Haan said. "They are in control of the entire Northeast Corridor."

"That's impossible," the station manager said.

"Please step outside," Agent Haan said curtly to the station manager. "This is now out of your hands."

The station manager didn't appear to be willing to do anything of the sort, but the heavily armed Agent Haan fixed him with a cold stare and he threw his hands up and walked out.

"They definitely have Snap and access to certain government systems," Senator Carol Redstone said.

Diana shook her head. "But why! They're good kids, I just don't understand why."

"We can't waste any more time here," agent Haan said. "They can run that train at eight hundred kph until the vacuum tunnel ends in Hartford or Boston. Boston is the terminus for the coastal rout, but if they go inland to Hartford, the line continues on land through Vermont and well into Canada. We can track the train by infrared satellite until it comes above ground. I have a Stealth AV flyer waiting on the roof. If we leave now we can intercept them in less than thirty minutes." Then agent Haan fixed Diana with a stern look. "The question that only you must be able to answer, Dr. Saint Sommers, are they going to Boston or Hartford?"

Diana didn't know why, but she had a feeling that Boston was not their destination. It would be perilous for her to lie to Agent Haan, who likely had voice analyzers charting every word they spoke. Sighing, she said in a very small voice, "I don't know. But I have a feeling they'll go inland."

Senator Redstone nodded her head. "Agent Haan. Have you located Theodora Devereaux?"

"Of course," agent Haan replied. "She is being held for questioning."

"Get her," Redstone said. "We'll have to bring her with us and question her en route."

Austrian was seated at a dining table in the second car of the seven-car train. The kids seemed much more mature and sure of themselves than he had expected. Mary Wang and Jason Solvet were seated opposite him while Deque rummaged through the café cupboards.

"I hope Dr. Saint Sommers isn't in too much trouble," Mary said.

"It's only going to take us a day to do this whole thing," Deque replied, his head buried in a food storage compartment. "Then nobody will be in trouble because the whole world will have changed."

Austrian looked up at the ceiling. He could sense where they were, but wanted to show some vulnerability and allow the kids to take the lead for as long as possible. "Where are we?" he asked.

Jason looked out the window at the blurred tunnel wall speeding by. "Snap?"

A smooth voice sounded over the train's PA system. "You are currently passing New Haven station. You will arrive at Hartford station in less than twelve minutes. When you exit the vacuum tunnel in Hartford and travel along the above-ground tracks, I will have to reduce the train's speed to two hundred seventy kilometers per hour or risk derailment."

"That means we'll be in Vermont at White River Junction in less than an hour," Jason said. "Dr. Merryweather will pick us up there and take us to his bee farm."

Austrian looked up at the ceiling again. It was important for these kids to think in a dynamic nature, to expect to have to adapt to changing circumstances. "I'm not sure... I'm not sure everything is going to go the way we planned."

Deque popped out of the café with a sandwich in his hand. "Why the hell do you say that? We're smarter than you, and we made this whole plan. We didn't even need you to come with us, we just needed you to get Snap. And anyway, you're too old to even understand how the conversion formulas work. You don't understand how any of this works. So why are you saying our plan isn't going to work?"

Mary frowned at Deque. "Stop being a jerk, Deque. Austrian was the one who had Snap contact us. He told us about the Merryweather sequence. This was all his idea to begin with."

Pleased that the kids were willing to argue and take sides, Austrian decided to show them how plans could change. "Deque's right. I don't understand how we can make the dodecahedron work." Austrian looked up at the ceiling again. "They're after us already. We didn't get enough of a head start."

Snap's voice came over the PA system. "Austrian is correct. I just monitored a flight plan authorized by Homeland Defense. An anti-terrorist classified flyer called a Stealth AV is in pursuit of us. At its present speed, it will intercept us somewhere between Springfield and Greenfield, Massachusetts."

Deque slammed his fist against a wall. "Shit. We would have had more time if we hadn't stopped to pick him up," he said, glaring at Austrian.

"Snap?" Mary asked. "How do they know we're not going to Boston? Didn't you cancel the Acela train routing system?"

"Perhaps they are able to track us via infrared satellite. I am currently working to disable those satellites," Snap replied.

Austrian shook his head. "It doesn't matter. Diana Saint Sommers knows you all too well. She has a sense of what you will do."

"Is Dr. Saint Sommers in the plane?" Mary asked.

Snap gave them the rundown. "The Stealth AV crew consists of Diana Saint Sommers, Senator Carol Redstone, TVCom representative Theodora Devereaux, and FBI Special Agent Haan. Psychological profile of Senator Redstone indicates a seventy nine percent probability that she will use force to stop this train after a brief negotiations period. I am unable to locate information about Special agent Haan."

"Shit, this is his fault," Deque said, looking at Austrian. "They'll just blow up the train."

Austrian decided he would have to show them how to be dynamic. It seemed they needed an example of innovation and some reason to keep following him. Austrian thought for a moment, then asked, "Snap, what are the major landmarks we'll pass between here and White River Junction in Vermont?"

"You will cross three medium span bridges, seven stations and a one point six kilometer tunnel under Mt. Pomfret two kilometers before White River Junction," Snap said.

Austrian nodded. It seemed appropriate to sound just a little bit smug. "Then there's a very simple way we can throw them off our trail."

9

RUNAWAY TRAIN

The Stealth AV made it to Hartford, Connecticut ten minutes after the hijacked train. Debris scattered the tracks where the train had smashed through the air locks and passed onto the above ground rails without stopping. A large group of police cars and officers surrounded the scene.

Diana held back her sigh of relief. She needed to figure out a way to stall, a chance to talk to the kids before this Agent Haan did something drastic.

The Stealth flyer never stopped. "We will intercept the train forty miles north of Springfield, Massachusetts," agent Haan said. "I recommend we target explosives on the engine once we have them in sight."

"No!" Diana yelled. "You can't fire on three children! Good heavens, are you crazy? Let me talk to them!"

Senator Redstone nodded. "Federal protocol demands that a negotiations attempt must be made before we can legally use force. And we have to be particularly prudent as our use of force will impact an interstate transportation infrastructure."

"I'm sure if I can talk to them we can figure all this craziness out," Diana said in a tempo that augmented her persuasiveness.

"Fine, but I'm not giving you a lot of time. This is a matter of national security and we will take every measure possible to ensure that our work does not escape our ability to control."

Haan pointed to a display. "Why are there four people on that train? Our satellite is detecting four people. One is an adult male."

A squawk escaped Theodora Devereaux. "My assistant! Austrian Tyrol. I never found him when we evacuated. He's obviously been tricked since he's simply not smart enough to know better. It's our human resources department. They're supposed to screen out potentially troubled applicants. I had reservations about hiring him, but they said he was an ideal candidate. Ideal! My old programming assistant got some strange illness I think was all in her head. Left just like that so I was in a pinch. I have never taken a sick day in all my life."

Carol Redstone fixed Theodora with a dubious stare. "Are you sure he's the only one at the TVCom League 'in cahoots' with those kids? At this point I would say that you are an accomplice in defrauding the American government. Just what exactly was that Snap persona created to do?"

"Whaaat! I am certainly not involved in any illegal activity. And as for our Snap project, I am not at liberty to discuss confidential TVCom work," Theodora said decisively. "I am under no obligation to answer your questions!"

The cockpit display screen suddenly went blank. "They have control of our satellites," Haan said.

A girl's voice came over the stealth's com channel. "Dr. Saint Sommers? It's me, Mary."

"Mary?" Diana called. "Mary what in seven heaven are you kids doing? You're scaring us all very much."

"Dr. Saint Sommers, we're going to St. Albans in Vermont." Mary answered. Diana could tell Mary was fibbing. That wasn't going to please that severe Agent Haan.

"Mary, this is Senator Carol Redstone. If you stop this train right now, you won't get into any trouble."

"Yes we will." It was Deque's voice.

Diana was about to answer when Senator Redstone held up her hand, indicating she was to control this discussion. She straightened her face and asked, "What is it that you want?"

There was silence on the other end for a moment. Then Mary said, "We've kidnapped Austrian Tyrol."

Theodora Devereaux jumped up and stuck her face where she thought a microphone might be. "Austrian? Are you there? Don't tell those kids anything. You don't want to breech the confidentiality agreement you signed. See what happens when you go into those trances! You end up getting kidnapped by children!"

There was a muffled sound. Mary said, "He can't talk. We have him gagged. He accidentally found out stuff about our work when he was programming Snap. We think Austrian is really smart like almost as smart as us. He understands all about the Saint Sommers formula and how to apply it to the spectrum modulations."

"Oh, you can't be serious, Mary," Diana Saint Sommers said. What was Mary up to? Diana realized Mary was doing the same thing she was—buying time. The longer they talked, the longer they prevented an attack on the train. Diana jumped back into the conversation before Redstone could. "Mary, I'm really confused why you would kidnap someone. That's not like you at all, Mary. You give me one good reason why you would do such a silly thing."

"Well, he, uhm, he kidnapped us first," Mary said. "He told us he'd ruin our whole project if we didn't meet him at Union Station. So we met him on the empty train, like he told us to, but then the train took off and he said Snap was in control and the train wouldn't stop until we reached St. Albans. Then that was when Jason and Deque jumped him and gagged him and tied him up in case he was going to try to hurt us."

"What is in St. Albans?" Carol Redstone asked.

"We don't know," Mary said.

"Take the gag off him. He won't hurt you," Theodora said.

"Yes! For heaven's sake, Mary," Diana pleaded.

"Oh, no, we're too scared," Mary said. "But anyway, before we gagged him, he said that his boss, Theodora

Devereaux was really smart and she knew everything, too. And that she knew what was in St. Albans."

Diana almost smiled as she heard Mary deliver that curveball.

"Is this true?" Carol Redstone asked Theodora. "How much do you know about our spectrum modulations work?"

Theodora sputtered for a few moments. "As I previously stated, I am not at liberty to discuss what I know or understand. As for St. Albans, I have no idea what is there."

"I don't believe you for a moment," Redstone said.

"Austrian?" Theodora said. "Austrian, I really *really* do not know what is in St. Albans, do I?" She asked it like she might be expecting some hint from him.

Mary answered, "Sorry, he's still gagged. Uh, oh, I think that Snap thing is cutting off our communications. Please try to stay with us until we reach St. Albans." The speaker went dead.

Deque laughed hysterically after they cut the com channel. Jason frowned at him and Mary just let out a big sigh.

"Well done," Austrian said. "We gained approximately seventy five seconds."

"Are you sure your boss doesn't understand the St. Sommers formula?" Jason asked Austrian.

Austrian nodded. "She was one of the rare people who once had the capacity. It was a danger to our project, so as you understand, I took care of it. But as her mind struggles with the blocks that I put in place, they cause her to be unstable. Fortunately, she is predictable."

"Well, as long as they don't try anything until we get off, then we'll be okay," Deque said.

"We're going to have to walk two kilometers to White River Junction," Jason said. "We'll be late meeting Dr. Merryweather. How do we know he's gonna wait for us?"

"He's very reliable and very patient and very much intent on us succeeding," Austrian said. "He will wait for us."

"I suggest you all move to the rear coach," Snap said. "We will soon be passing under Mt. Pomfret."

Deque pointed with his sandwich and they all began making their way to the rear car. "If this doesn't work, we're completely screwed," he said.

Austrian drew a symbol in the air and stared at blank space for a minute. "It will work."

Diana didn't like that sour look on Agent Haan's face after their talk with Mary.

"The voice analysis reports a one hundred percent probability that Mary Wang was lying the entire duration of her transmission," Agent Haan said. "In the interest of national security, I recommend disabling the train's main engine."

"What in the world is so important that you need to derail a train and kill children?" Diana demanded.

"Probability of injury in the resulting derailment is estimated at sixteen percent," Agent Haan said. "The train is equipped with styro-gel emergency restraints leaving very little probability of death. My official recommendation is to disable the train. They have followed a classic terrorist strategy of delaying and supplying us with misinformation. If we continue to follow the train to St. Albans, they will already have done whatever it is that they are going to do."

"Can we broadcast a message to them?" Carol Redstone asked. "Will they hear it?"

"If we broadcast on several upper frequencies, the train's PA system will pick up the transmission and they will hear us," Agent Haan reported.

"Then do it," Redstone said. "Warn them that if they do not immediately stop the train we will fire on the main engine and they will get hurt."

"Oh my God, no!" Diana yelled. "That's a monstrous thing to do!" Diana watched the train on the display. She realized why Mary needed to buy that time. But Diana was determined to keep them from firing, just in case their trick didn't work.

"Well, Diana," Carol said with a smirk, "They told us Snap was in control of the train and we're just trying to save them." She nodded to Agent Haan. "Do it."

"Just one moment," Haan said. "They are entering the Mt. Pomfret tunnel. They will not receive the message until they have cleared the mountain."

Ten seconds later, the train zipped out of the tunnel and Haan broadcast her message. "If you are able to stop the train we recommend that you do so now or we will fire on the main engine and you will derail and risk injury or death."

There was no response. "I don't think they heard you," Diana said. "You should try that again."

"Oh, they heard you" Carol said. "Warn them that you will fire, and then do it."

"This is your last warning. Stop the train or we will fire on the engine."

No response. Haan and Redstone exchanged a silent communication. "Targeting engine," Agent Haan said.

Diana lunged between the weapons console and Agent Haan, using her body as a barricade. "There is just no way that I will allow you to do this."

Agent Haan fixed Diana with a solid glare. "Step to the side, Dr. Saint Sommers."

Diana grabbed the seat. "I'm not moving."

"Listen, Diana," Senator Redstone said. "This is as much for their safety as that of the country." Redstone motioned Haan to remove Diana.

Haan stood, wrapped her arms around Diana's midsection and hauled her out of the cockpit. Though she had the breath knocked out of her, Diana jumped back up and hurled herself toward the cockpit.

Carol blocked Diana as Haan retook her seat. "I am firing a low yield EM disturbance probe at the engine."

A small rocket launched off the stealth and sped along side the train, pacing the engine car. Once the weapon exactly matched the train's velocity, it maneuvered to within one inch of the forward car and burst, emitting a bright flash of electromagnetic radiation. The main engine immediately seized, slid along the track for a brief moment, then the rear cars buckled, derailed and jumped forward in an accordion pattern. Huge tracks of earth were gouged out of the ground as the massive cars slid sideways and then flipped over one another, barreling into the earth at two hundred kilometers per hour.

As the flyer hovered and landed next to the wreck, Diana Saint Sommers silently sobbed, looking below through a huge cloud of dust and smoke at the mangled mass of torn metal and smashed glass.

10

INTO THE WOOD

The moment the last car of the train entered the tunnel, Snap disengaged it, allowing the rest of the train to continue on to smoothly exit on the other side, showing that it clearly had not stopped or slowed at any point in the tunnel. The detached car was then stopped and the kids got out.

Snap's voice shouted to them from the train. "Run along the forest to the left. There's a road that leads to White River Junction. Meanwhile, I'm going to buy you some more time by hiding this train coach."

As the children ran to the tunnel exit, Snap maneuvered the train backwards along the track and switched it to an ancient, out of use line. Then the train moved forward, started to turn along the track, and smashed through a boarded up side of the tunnel, where it fell three hundred feet into an abandoned mine.

A moment after they heard the muffled sound of the car thudding to the bottom of the mine, a huge cloud of dust appeared along the horizon at the end of the tunnel.

"Look at that," Mary said, and they could see the train cars flipping over one another in the distance. "Oh my God, they blew up the train."

"Keep moving," Deque said. "They're going to be after us soon."

Mary started running to the other end of the tunnel. Jason and the others followed and then they were all running toward daylight. Once outside the tunnel, Deque led the charge, crashing through the brush and into the forest.

"You'll need to turn about ten degrees to your left," Snap said over the speaker on Deque's iWatch. Deque made the adjustment and they continued to run for another ten minutes until they emerged, panting, sweaty and covered with twigs onto a deserted country road.

Deque called up a map. "We just have to head north on this road for about two kilometers and we'll be at White River Junction."

They started walking at a brisk pace. The sun was about two hours from setting. The calm air and chirping birds flitting among the trees were a surreal contrast to the mad train ride and sense of danger they all felt. Deque shook his head. "This is going to take us too long."

Jason nodded. "They're going to realize really soon that we got off in the tunnel and they can probably find us real easy."

"Snap, can you tell if they're still at the train wreck?" Deque asked.

There was no response.

"Snap?"

"He should be able to contact us anywhere," Mary said.

"Duh!" Jason said. "They've figured it out. They know we got off the train, and they've done something to keep us from talking to anyone."

Deque switched apps on his watch. "There's a lot of distortion on all frequencies. There's a scrambler blanketing this whole area. Probably for more than a hundred square kilometers."

A low hum filled the air. "It's the Stealth!" Deque said.

The group stood frozen for moments, each one expecting the flyer to appear above them at any moment. Running into the woods would provide no more protection than the open road. It would be an easy thing for the flyer to scan the deserted country side for four individuals.

Austrian had closed his eyes and was humming to himself in some sort of trance. After a moment he said, "Follow me," and walked into the woods on the other side of the road.

The children followed. "They can still find us in here," Deque said. "If we run down the road it'll only take us ten minutes."

"That's not enough time," Austrian said. "Just keep following me."

The forest quickly turned to muck left over from the spring thaw. "Where are we going?" Jason asked.

The hum from the stealth flyer was growing closer. "I see it!" Mary shouted.

A black shape could be seen zigzagging among the treetops less than half a kilometer away. The flyer seemed to be honing in on their general area, but wasn't headed straight toward them.

"Why haven't they spotted us?" Deque asked.

Suddenly they heard a gruff female voice shouting from a clearing ahead of them. "What are you still doing out here? Everyone was supposed to be back half an hour ago!"

"Who's that?" Mary whispered.

Austrian led the group to the dirt-packed clearing where they heard the voice. A beefy woman wearing a whistle and a sweatshirt that said, "Camp Lakewood," walked toward Austrian and shook her finger at him. "All camp councilors were supposed to get back from the hike an hour ago," the woman said. As she got a closer look at Austrian and the children, the woman stopped. "Who are you?"

Austrian fixed his eyes on the woman and walked toward her. She seemed terrified for a moment, frozen, unable to take a step. A small groan escaped her throat.

Austrian continued to approach the woman then stood in front of her. "You remember us. We got lost. You have come to help us."

The woman's body went limp, eyelids drooping. Her eyes suddenly snapped open and she said, "What's the matter? You get lost?"

"Sorry. We got lost," Austrian said.

The woman frowned at him. "You should wear some more sensible cloths than that. What the devil is that sound?" The woman scanned the sky. The flyer was close, but couldn't be seen any longer.

"Uhm, which way do we go?" Austrian asked.

The woman shook her head, apparently disgusted with Austrian's lack of woodland skills. "Come on."

The group was led down a short trail and emerged into a grassy square surrounded by cabins where there were about fifty kids playing games and eating hot dogs. The woman left them among the kids and joined a cluster of adults.

"What now?" Deque asked.

Just then, the flyer roared among the treetops and hovered over the camp. Kids screamed as a hot cyclone of air blasted over them. "Keep your heads down," Austrian said. "If they can't see our faces they can't isolate us from the others."

The group crouched for an insufferable amount of time. Finally, the flyer moved out of the space directly above them and began setting down in a nearby soccer field.

"We have to get out of here," Deque said.

Jason nodded and grabbed the closest screaming kid. "Which way are the railroad tracks?" he asked.

The boy stared at him blankly, then squirmed to get away.

Jason shook the boy. "Which way are the railroad tracks?" he yelled.

"Over there!" the boy shouted.

One of the adults was yelling. "Everyone get into the cabins!"

As the camp full of children ran for their cabins it was easy for Jason, Mary, Deque and Austrian to head off back into the woods in the direction the boy had indicated.

One minute away from the camp, the sound of the flyer was gone, indicating it had landed. The group ran a few minutes until they found the tracks. Deque hastily checked his map and led them in the right direction.

"It'll take them a while to search the camp," Mary panted.

It was a frantic fifteen minute run. Somewhere several kilometers ahead of them, they could hear fire engine sirens. "People must have found the train wreck," Jason said.

Another minute on the track and they came to a road. An elderly man standing next to a white van waved to them.

"Quick, get into the van," he said.

There were no hellos until they were speeding down the road.

"I saw the train barrel through here and that fancy jet following it a while back," the old man said. "Darndest thing I ever saw. They blew it right off the tracks. Glad to see you kids made it."

"Everyone, I'd like you to meet Dr. Maxtone Merry-weather," Austrian said.

In the back seat, Mary threw up.

11

THE HUNT

The Stealth flyer had just put down in a clearing next to the train wreck when Theodora Devereaux said, "Weeell. What happened to the last car? There were seven cars and now there are only six!"

Haan scanned the train. "There is a program running that is sending out simulated electromagnetic biosignatures."

"Damn!" Carol Redstone cursed and stormed out of the flyer, followed by Agent Haan. After a brief search of the wreck, they reentered the flyer.

"They weren't on the train," Agent Haan said.

"Oh thank God!" Diana sighed. "You would have killed them and I would have made sure you ended up in prison."

Carol cast an irritated glance at Diana. "Find them," she said to Agent Haan.

Agent Haan scanned through some maps on the Stealth dash, looking for thermogenic traces that would suggest the recent presence of people. She found none. "I suggest we not waste time stopping at the Mount Pomfret tunnel," Agent Haan said. "They would not still be there."

"Agreed," Redstone said.

The flyer took off and in a moment was hovering over Mt. Pomfret. Had the circumstances been different, anyone aboard the flyer might have enjoyed the panoramic view of the rolling green hills specked with the first yellow leaves of fall, the countryside dotted with white church steeples. But no one was looking out the windows. All eyes were trained on a display screen.

Four red shapes appeared on the display.

"There they are," Agent Haan said.

She maneuvered the flyer in the direction of the children, when a fifth shape appeared on the screen.

"Who's that?" Carol Redstone asked.

"Not a child," Agent Haan said. "Probably the person they planned to meet."

As the display followed the five shapes, twenty more bodies appeared, then more.

"Which ones are they? Can you isolate them?" Carol asked.

"Scanning for facial matches," Haan said. "I can no longer get a physical profile match since not all the faces are in view. If we take the flyer low enough to use resonance for biometric confirmation, it will kill the people below."

"Why don't you just shoot them all?" Diana said sarcastically. "I mean, for the love of Pete, you're so darned eager to kill children!"

The jibe was lost on Theodora. "If you aim at their legs you won't kill them," she suggested.

Agent Haan ignored both women. "We will set down and sweep the camp. Even if we lose the kids, we'll likely be able to find out what they were after."

By the time the four women made it to the camp, all the children had been hidden away in the cabins. A group of adults met the woman on the camp commons.

Agent Haan held up her ID. "I'm FBI Special Agent Haan. We are looking for three children by the names of Deque Demarquez, Jason Solvet and Mary Wang. They are accompanied by a man in his twenties named Austrian Tyrol."

"We don't have anyone in the camp by those names," a man said.

A bulky woman wearing a sweatshirt and whistle stepped forward. "Wait a minute, I found three kids and a young man just a few minutes ago. I thought they were stragglers."

"What was the man wearing?" Theodora asked.

"He was dressed in fancy business clothes," the woman said.

"Are they still here?" Agent Haan asked.

"Damned if I know," the woman said. "What's this all about? There been a killin'?"

Haan squinted at the woman. "Ma'am, if you are lying to us it is a federal offense. You will be charged with aiding and abetting a criminal who has crossed state lines with minors."

The woman crossed her arms and said, "I said I don't know anything about it."

Agent Haan checked her voice analyzer and reported that the woman was telling the truth. She then removed a small device that made a "ping" noise. "There are several children that could be your students, but no adult male confirmed matches within range." Next, Haan took a small metal cylinder the size of a pen and pushed it into the ground. She "pinged" the ground and reported, "There are two carboment cellars beneath those cabins." Haan nodded to her companions. "Theodora, come with me. We'll take this one, you two search the other." Haan handed Senator Redstone a sidearm.

"Oh, for pity sake put that away," Diana said as she ran after Carol.

The search took an hour. Agent Haan had them examine all the cabins, inventoried the children and searched for trap doors, crawl spaces, storage rooms and secret bunkers. Diana was torn between comforting crying kids and keeping up with Carol. Agent Haan then began an interrogation of each member of the camp. The fifth boy she questioned said that a strange boy asked where the railroad tracks were. It didn't take voice analysis to see that the crying boy was telling the truth.

Theodora's phone rang. "Hello?"

"Theodora. It's Jordan Bliss. I want an update."

Theodora moved off to an isolated area. "I'm in Vermont. Those crazy kids stole a train and my assistant is with them. We followed them on some trumped up military jet, but they got away."

"Who's "we"?" Jordan Bliss asked.

"Who? Well, there's that scientist woman, Diana Saint Sommers. I really don't know how she won a Nobel Prize. And there's Senator Redstone and some tall person, I think she's a woman, from the FBI."

Jordan Bliss grunted. "An FBI agent, a senator, a Nobel Prize winning scientist and a military jet, and they didn't catch those kids? This has got to be some kind of ruse. Are they surprised you got a call? I had to use some high powered equipment to get this call to you. Some kind of high tech interference wherever the hell you are. Look it, I got about seventy lawyers looking at whether or not we can use the Terrorist Act of 2027 as a precedent to declare war on the government."

Theodora squawked. "Whaaat? You're going to have the TVCom League declare war on the U.S. Government?"

"That's right," Bliss said bluntly. "Hal's lookin' at me like I got horns, but I want to know everything you can about that jet you're using. Specs, weapons, shielding, everything. Send the info on a TVCom secured channel to my office in Dunedin. Goodbye."

The phone went dead. Theodora shrugged.

She rejoined the women and Agent Haan eyed her suspiciously. "How were you able to get a call?

Theodora smiled and waved her hands at the sky. "We have our ways. I am a senior executive of the TVCom League."

Agent Haan made a noise that warned Theodora that mistrust had just gone up a notch.

Carol Redstone waved a hand at their surroundings. "We're done here. Back to the flyer. We have to sweep the countryside for those kids."

Once back in the Stealth AV, agent Haan scrolled through several map schematics. After unsuccessfully trying to access some FBI directories, Haan turned to Theodora and held up a gloved hand. "Tell me how you are able to communicate through the ionic distortions."

Theodora looked around as if Haan was speaking to another person.

"You received a phone call from Chairman Jordan Bliss. Only the TVCom League can generate that level frequency. So tell me or I will be forced to make you tell me."

"Whaat?" Theodora screeched. "Are you threatening me with torture? That is a criminal violation of amendment..."

Dr. Diana Saint Sommers cut her off. "Oh for the love of Pete you can see Ms. Devereaux has no means to answer you! You might need some voice analyzer to tell you if she's lying but the C minor of her speech is consistent and she's obviously just as confounded as I am. You cannot bully and threaten United States citizens! And you," Diana said, turning to Senator Redstone. "You would threaten your reelection next year with illegal tactics? Why, that's just how Senator Tricarical lost his seat!"

Agent Haan had lost interest in their conversation and was pulling up other schematics on her screen. "I have no access to satellite imaging taken within the last ten hours. However, there is still an isolated state traffic camera system. These pictures were taken on route 89, recorded forty minutes ago."

The screen displayed several stills of a white van with three children and a young man who appeared to be Austrian. The children and Austrian are shown running toward the van, piling and speeding down the highway.

Agent Haan identified the vehicle tag and received route information. "The vehicle is reported to have traveled west of here. It is registered to this address in the town of Burlington at a site on the southern portion of Lake Champlain."

Ten minutes later the Stealth AV had arrived at Burlington and identified the location of the van. The Stealth was set on quiet mode and set down out of earshot, about half a kilometer away from the large lakeside compound identified as number 13 Harrison Avenue.

"Stay behind me," Agent Haan directed as they approached the house. A metal gate with an intercom blocked their entrance. Haan held up a gloved hand and pressed her finger against the intercom. A low beep sounded and the gate began to slide open.

Children's voices could be heard coming from the front of the house.

Diana suddenly stopped in her tracks at the sound of the voices.

Agent Haan looked at Diana. "Your galvanic skin responses have suddenly changed."

"Oh my heavens, have they?" Diana asked.

Haan looked irritated. "You three stay against this wall."

The women did as they were told.

Haan drew her weapon and walked onto the lawn. "FBI! Everyone stay where you are and put your hands where I can see them!"

Three children, a young man, and an older man suddenly turned toward Haan.

"Who are you?" the older man called. "What is this about?"

"I said put your hands in the air and do not move!" Agent Haan repeated. It was getting dark, and difficult to make out the people on the lawn, so Haan kept her weapon aimed at the older man.

The man put his hands in front of him and spoke to the children. "Okay, okay. Kids, just stay still—I'm sure this is some mistake."

"Move toward me, slowly," Agent Haan commanded.

As they moved closer to the FBI agent, Haan called back to the women. "Dr. Saint Sommers, Senator, Theodora, please verify identity."

The women approached behind agent Haan. In front of them, a girl, two boys, a young man and an older man slowly approached. The girl was holding a plate of hot dogs. The two boys each held long barbeque forks they were fencing with moments ago. The older man and the younger man each held a glass of wine.

Senator Redstone swore. "It's not them."

Theodora squawked. "That's not Austrian! Some system you have at the FBI!"

Haan lowered her weapon.

The man approached her. "What the hell is this all about?"

Agent Haan looked at the man. "It is too unlikely a coincidence that you so closely resemble the group of people we are looking for. Where are Austrian Tyrol, Mary Wang, Deque Demarquez, and Jason Solvet?"

The man looked puzzled. "I've never heard of those people in my life. You said you're FBI?"

Diana looked at Agent Haan. "Well he clearly has not heard of them! You apologize! Oh, never mind." Diana march up to the older man and said, "I am so sorry this was just a terrible mistake. You see I run a school and some of my students went missing and well, angels don't weep except when children are in trouble. So you see we've just been looking for them and we were so excited to have finally found them and, oh, her," Diana said, looking at Agent Haan. "Well, you know, it was possibly a matter of interstate kidnapping so the FBI, bless them, offered to help. I'm Diana Saint Sommers."

"THE Diana Saint Sommers?" the man asked, squinting his eyes to get a better look. "Well I'll be!"

Diana tilted her head bashfully. "Well if you mean the musician, yes, I am."

The man smiled, "Well I'll be twice! My name is Robert Shukizo. My brother wrote that biography about you last year!"

Diana gasped. "Well if this isn't the smallest world!"

Haan interrupted. "Mr. Shukizo. Can you explain why you were picking up these children outside of White River Junction this afternoon?"

Robert Shukizo did not appear to be pleased to answer Haan's question. "You want me to explain why I was picking up my son and grandchildren?" Shukizo asked. "Hmmm, let me see..." he said sarcastically. "They were at the grocery store, buying food for a cookout... I guess I could have made them walk sixty miles to my house, but I decided to give them a ride!"

Haan continued, undaunted. "Why on this date? Did someone ask you to arrange this family affair?"

At this point, the younger man, who was apparently Mr. Shukizo's son and clearly closer to forty years old than Austrian's age stepped forward. "Kids, go into the house. You, ma'am, are trespassing on private property. We are not answering any questions until--" Flashing lights appeared around the house.

Carol Redstone grabbed Haan's arm and yanked her around. "Put your weapon away! This is going to take a hell of a lot of explaining so I suggest you contact your superiors while I talk to the police. Your bungling has put us very far behind!"

Theodora Devereaux nodded. "This is exactly why the government should not be meddling with the TVCom League! Inefficiencies!"

The back door to the house opened and a woman and three police officers exited.

"It's all right Tabitha, officers," Mr. Shukizo called. "Just a mistake."

A mistake that took two hours of phone calls, forms and explanations before the four women were escorted back to the Stealth AV.

Once back inside, Agent Haan defended her actions. "That was clearly a ruse." She fixed Diana with a stare. "You knew it was not them the instant you heard their voices, yet you continued to allow me to apprehend them." Haan then turned to Theodora. "And you want us to continue to believe you had no knowledge your assistant was working with these children?"

Senator Redstone cut off Haan. "Enough! Do not blame others for your incompetence!"

Agent Haan looked at the Senator with a deadly stare. "That man was clearly set up, and clearly unaware of it. This is an operation so vast, and," Haan pointed to Diana Saint Sommers, "It was coordinated right under your very nose at the Gifted Student Program you sponsored as Chair of the Spectrum committee."

Senator Redstone opened her phone. "I said enough of this. The FBI director has given me until the morning to resolve this matter. Then he turns it over to Homeland IST. At which point I no longer have a career. And I will see to it that you do not either. So I suggest resuming the search!"

Theodora and Diana exchanged glances. They were both under suspicion and suspicious of each other. And both at the mercy of two desperate people.

It was going to be a dangerous night.

12

MAXTONE MERRYWEATHER

Jason, Mary and Deque were very businesslike when they arrived at Dr. Merryweather's farm. Where are the bees? How do we construct the dodecahedron array? How long will this take?

Maxtone Merryweather wasn't one to be rushed. And Austrian was the type of person who never felt hurried or nervous no matter what the circumstances. So after the winding hour long drive through the Vermont hills to the farm, Dr. Merryweather's wife made them all sit and have tea and blueberry pie.

"They're still looking for us, you know," Deque said.

"And you know Dr. Saint Sommers--she'll tell them we're here," Mary said.

Austrian shook his head. "I don't think Dr. Saint Sommers is going to help them find you. She is obviously concerned for your safety, but she will not turn you over to the FBI, even if she does suspect you have come to see Dr. Merryweather. I also suspect Dr. Merryweather's farm is not so easy to find, even with a Stealth AV flier."

"Is that true?" Deque asked.

Dr. Merryweather dismissed the children's questions and talked about rain.

"There's really nothing more pleasant than rain during a summer day. I like to walk out barefoot on the grass," Merryweather mused.

Dorothy Merryweather frowned. "Then he'll come in covered in mud and fall asleep on the couch."

"Better to lie in mud than on that synthetic fabric," Maxtone Merryweather said. "That's natural. Don't you kids like to play in the rain?"

The children looked at him like he had two heads.

"I guess they've got you working so much you missed out on that. Well, they're calling for rain tomorrow. All the robins will come out to eat their worms and we can enjoy it all with them."

By this point, Mary had sized up the situation and decided to employ her charm to get things rolling. "Dr.

Merryweather, I think the sunset is beautiful. Could you give a tour before dark?"

"We should hurry. That jet could find us any minute," Deque said.

Merryweather dismissed the comment with a wave of his hand. "Not to worry. We have ways of dealing with that if it happens. And you will need to sleep before leaving here. It has been a long day. They won't find us until tomorrow."

"How do you know that?" Deque asked. "And what if they do? Do you have weapons here? Because that's what it will take."

Dr. Merryweather smiled. "My dear boy, we are protected by nature. That's the best weapon ever devised."

Jason and Deque exchanged annoyed glances. "What do you mean by that? You have some big tree that can fire lasers strong enough to knock a Stealth out of the sky?"

Mrs. Merryweather shook her finger at her husband. "Ted, stop being so damned cavalier. They're kids, they're frightened, and you aren't helping them with your nonsense."

"Oh, I'm sorry. I really am being insensitive," Dr. Merryweather said. "Yes, I do have weapons that can protect us.

And they're based on very powerful *natural* laws. You kids are doing something extraordinarily brave and important for humanity. I'm sorry for being so unempathetic."

Austrian cleared his throat. "Dr. Merryweather, if I may. The anxiety of being pursued has had a detrimental impact on Mary, Jason and Deque. The three of them need calm and concentration. It would be helpful if you explain why we are safe here."

Merryweather nodded. "Indeed. I have been waiting for this day for many years." Merryweather stood and looked out the window. "When Austrian told me the final details of the plan, we made assumptions about pursuit and detection. Snap will have taken off-line most of recent satellite images. So they will have to resort to on the ground reconnaissance. I happen to know where the old highway traffic cameras are. Shortly after picking you up, two other vans in different locations within a one mile radius of white river junction also picked up three children and one young man. Both caught on traffic cameras. They have driven to two different locations across the state, and they are unaware that it was me who arranged it. It will be difficult for the FBI agent to track down every lead, and it will take them some time to realize the ruse. That buys us a few hours. At that time a sequence of energy readings will be deployed and detected by them at some very inconvenient locations. Then there is a variation of search patterns they can employ that will eventually lead them here."

Merryweather turned to the kitchen table. "Austrian was very thorough about the algorithm. Within a standard deviation of two hours, it will take a minimum of ten hours to locate this farm. By that time, we will be long gone."

A quiet pause settled over the kitchen as everyone caught their breath. Dr. Merryweather said, "Okay, why don't we go see my bees before the sun sets. That is the best time to begin your calibrations."

Dr. Merryweather led them on a walk through an ancient apple orchard. Clusters of mayflies and moths hovered in the last rays of sunlight that shone through the tree branches as the white petals from the last of summer's flower blossoms fluttered down around them. At the end of the orchard was a grassy field with a city of wooden boxes. The black silhouettes of bees buzzed above the hives.

"Here we are," Dr. Merryweather said.

Deque started scratching his arms. "Shouldn't we put on those beekeeper net-outfit things?"

Merryweather reached into his pocket and pulled out four tiny cubes. He handed one to each of them. "Just put one of these in your pockets and they won't bother you."

"I haven't had a chance to fully explain how the bees work," Austrian said. "I was only able to give them the general idea."

Dr. Merryweather smiled. "Oh good. A lesson. You see, bees don't have much for brains, only a few million neurons. But when a bee finds food, he comes back to the hive and does a dance that tells the other bees the angle of the sun over the horizon, and the angle of the food to the hive, allowing them to triangulate on the source of the food. So how do they encode so much information on such tiny brains?"

Mary demurely raised her hand.

"Yes, you in the yellow shirt."

Mary kept her facial expressions calm and delightful while she played along. "We studied the ways bees talk after Snap told us about Austrian's plan. The bees have some way of detecting Earth's magnetic field. So all they have to do is know three things. The position of the sun, how far away the sun is from the horizon, and their position in the earth's magnetic field."

"Excellent," Dr. Merryweather said. "But the question is, how do they know where they are in the earth's magnetic field?"

"No one ever figured that out," Mary said.

Dr. Merryweather raised his hand. "I did." He gently lowered his hand to the edge of a hive and allowed a bee to crawl along his fingers. "You see, a little bee like this fellow can detect the quantum levels of physics. They can sense quarks. They can sense variations in the earth's magnetic field and the polarization of the sun's light. That's how they get those three bits of vital information. But the key is that those three bits of information must be decoded, the bee must have a means of communicating it to the other bees. But the other bees weren't there. They didn't detect those quantum variations themselves. So the bee performs a complex dance that decodes the information. It is very similar to the way a computer decompresses a compressed file. The bee's dance follows the shape of a hexagon in three dimensions. It's a shape known as the dodecahedron." Dr. Merryweather pointed to a barn. "The mechanism I designed is in there."

"It's small enough for us to just carry?" Deque asked.

Dr. Merryweather nodded. "There's a chamber inside that houses the bees. I've already isolated the ones you'll need to take."

Deque's iWatch spat out some static, then Snap's voice came through. "There has been a scrambler preventing me from getting through to you. I have successfully reconfigured a TVCom satellite to transmit on the Saint Sommers formula spectrum. Your device is receiving the signal and converting it with limited success, which is why my voice may sound strange."

"Hi Snap!" Mary said. "I didn't think we'd hear from you again until we were on our way to Florida."

"Speaking of that," Snap continued, "I have successfully accessed the SX-NASA controls. They will be available when you get to Kennedy-Carter Space Center. I have also been monitoring the Stealth Flyer. They are currently sixty miles west of here at the residence of a Robert Shukizo. Local police have been called to the residence."

Austrian squinted at the last rays of the setting sun. "We had better get to work." And with that, he led the group to Dr. Merryweather's laboratory.

Austrian opened his eyes after three hours of combative sleep. He was being attacked again. The voices from other universes knew he was close, getting closer to annihilating them. But he had learned to protect himself well and even in dreams they were not able to access his secrets.

A glint of sunlight shone through the window, the first rays of dawn had crept up to his chin, its angle over the trees showing that it was about 5:30. For a few moments upon waking, Austrian felt a strange sensation, the same sensation he had felt every morning for the past few months, the sensation of not having guilt over having used the kids in this way.

Guilt was for everyone else. Austrian was set on this path from the moment he was born. Mary, Jason and Deque were kids, even if they were smarter than the majority of adults, and as kids, they surely didn't have the deep sense of understanding about what they were doing.

To the kids and Dr. Merryweather, it simply appeared that Austrian had had his idea about Merryweather's work with bees and the Saint Sommers formulas for years. But there had been no way to transpose what the bees did to humans. To everyone else it appeared that Austrian was put on the Snap project by accident. That he accidentally learned about the broadcast spectrum, and had read about the Saint Sommers formula. All the missing pieces materialized before him. It was surely fate, he had convinced the children and Dr. Merryweather. The universe had delivered everything he needed. How could he not proceed? They all bought it. He was so close, but the voices attacking his mind were frantic. Time was running out. It was paramount he not show anxiety or give any clue as to the real purpose of this project.

Theodora had been the final and only obstacle. At one time, she would have been able to read the code and see what he was doing. But no longer. Austrian had made sure of that. "Just adding some necessary auxiliary code to the interfunctional matrix," he'd say when questioned about his work. Theodora liked talk like that. Soon, Snap's primary function switched from leading the TVCom debates in the U.S. Senate to creating immortality for humans.

Austrian had enjoyed telling Snap his childhood stories. After he had infiltrated the Gifted Student Program files and selected the necessary candidates, Austrian had enjoyed watching the children communicate with Snap and explain the stories to him like they would to a semi-sentient pet.

Once the children had grown to like and trust Snap, Austrian was able to reveal his plan to them. And Snap's unequaled powers of persuasion, powers programmed to convince the Supreme Court that the broadcast spectrum must be privately held, had worked just as well on the children to convince them that Austrian's plan was the most important thing ever to evolve in the history of humanity.

And it was. But not in the way they thought.

They didn't truly understand how this would fundamentally change what it was to be human. To be alive. To live. They did not understand what Dr. Diana Saint Sommers did when Dr. Merryweather had first approached her about his research. Diana Saint Sommers knew from the outset that what they were about to do was not meant for humanity, not at this time in evolution. And she was right. But whatever horrible fate befell humanity by the end of the day, if he was successful, then at least humanity would still exist.

Austrian wasn't entirely sure he understood the ramifications of his project on this world. Would it sink into horrible war? It didn't matter. There was The Great Issue at stake. Now, Diana Saint Sommers was the only person in this universe who had the power to stop him. The universe had demanded that he do it. It was not about what would be left of this world, it was about the survival of this universe.

So. Here he was.

He rose, got dressed, and woke the others.

Jason arrived in the kitchen and declared, "We need to get out of here."

Mrs. Merryweather sighed. Dr. Merryweather pointed to the table. "Have some juice and toast with honey. You have only had four hours of sleep and it is paramount you be alert."

They'd all worked through the night, making preparations, calibrating Merryweather's dodecahedron. The tension in the room was taut, and it seemed time for someone else to snap.

Austrian decided to speak. He didn't speak often, and he'd learned the less one speaks, the more they are listened to when they do speak.

"Jason, Mary and Deque. I think perhaps we have not spent enough time talking about what it is exactly that we are doing. So let's take a moment and consider everything. First, do you have any questions that I haven't covered?"

The children glanced at each other. Austrian realized that geniuses were sensitive and didn't like asking questions because it pointed to a weakness in their knowledge. He gave them time to think, raised his eyes earnestly at each one when it appeared they had a thought. Finally, Mary opened her mouth.

"What will it feel like?" she asked.

Austrian was perfectly honest. "I don't know. That's why when we get to the space station, I will be the first one to undergo the procedure. If it's successful and works the way we hope, then we will continue to perform the procedure on the entire planet."

Deque looked at the others, then shrugged and said, "I understand everything that we are doing, but how did all this start? I mean, who thought of this to begin with? Was it you, Dr. Merryweather?"

"I did the research," Dr. Merryweather said, "But it was Austrian's idea."

Austrian nodded. "A few years ago, after Dr. Merryweather finished fixing the mistakes from the second human genome project, he published some of his work about large strings of DNA that coded for inherited traits. The DNA provides large portions of the brain with information that we are not sure of, but that was assumed to be inherited personality and the like. But Dr. Merryweather noticed that a developing mind codes data in a pattern similar to the honeybee dance.

"Then I dreamed about it. I had visions of other lives. Past life experiences psychics would call it. But I immediately knew what it was. It was all the thoughts, feelings and experiences of all my ancestors. I realized I had the sum knowledge of all the thousands of people who led to my birth in my mind, but compressed, inaccessible. Just like the honeybee compresses its data.

"But how to access it? I would need the key to unlock that knowledge. The honeybee dodecahedron. I would need a way to activate the dodecahedron on that part of my brain. The Saint Sommers formula. And because this must not be a privilege accessible only to the elite, I would need a way to get it out to the whole world. I would need to broadcast the procedure to every living being. I would need access to a massive government communications array. Snap. I would need people who understood the Saint Sommers formula. Someone who could program the interface. Deque. Someone who could create a large enough frequency pipe to transmit to billions of people. Jason. And finally, someone who could divide that pipe into billions of individual broadcasts. Mary. And so, if we are successful, we will effectively resurrect every human being who has ever lived."

13

VECTOR

The sense that provided Austrian knowledge from the depths had shown him the FBI flyer reaching them before they left Dr. Merryweather's farm. Austrian briefly wondered how they would escape, but quickly put the thought out of his mind. Emergencies were to be dealt with when they occurred, not before.

After their brief breakfast, the group made their way to Dr. Merryweather's research laboratory: his barn. The weather-beaten slightly leaning structure was misleading. Inside, the walls and floor were a dark carbon composite and a maze of countertops were cluttered with electrical equipment The structure was completely impervious to outside interference from electricity or any frequency of light. Dr. Merryweather led the group to a black dodecahedron structure two feet across on one of the countertops.

"It is almost finished," Merryweather said. He pointed to some silver piping surrounding a glass inner chamber. "I have done as much with it as I can. This is the communication interface. You'll have to make the necessary adjustments, Deque, to get it to transmit on the Saint Sommers formula frequencies."

Deque studied it for a moment, then nodded. "This will take me exactly ten minutes." Deque searched through a nearby tool chest and went to work.

"I'll get the bee specimens," Merryweather said and disappeared among the maze of counters.

The kids hovered around Deque. "You're the slowest one of all of us," Jason said impatiently.

Deque paused a moment, looked up and said, "Shut up," then went back to his work.

Austrian explained, "The interface has to be calibrated to the highest frequency of the bee's quantum state. That occurs two hours after dawn."

Jason wrung his hands. "I told you the bandwidth I made could amplify that anyway!"

"Dr. Saint Sommers taught us that protocol for emergencies," Mary said to Jason. "This has to be done right so stop bothering everyone."

"I just want to get out of here and you're both so slow," Jason replied. "The second that Stealth flies over this farm they're going to notice this big building."

Mary showed Jason her handheld screen. "Look at this. There's a fusion reactor in the ground under here. I bet it can't be detected from outside."

"Wow. Dr. Merryweather must be rich to have one of those," Jason said.

Merryweather appeared with eight bees in a plastic container. "That was quite an expensive item to have built. The energy from that is what holds this floor together and powers the structure's shielding. Lets me keep a lot of things safe under there. The patents I have on over fourteen inventions keep the Mrs. and me living quite comfortably." Merryweather craned his arm around Deque and opened the dodecahedron's inner chamber, then attached the bee house. He tapped on the house until all the bees were transferred. "There. When you activate this the bees will each take a corner and then they'll do what they do. Now come and I'll show you to your transportation."

They followed Merryweather to the back of the barn. He opened a door and hit the lights. The rear room was a small aircraft hanger with a large military jet. "This is a Lockheed F-700, circa 2040. It's a bit old, but I have had it outfitted to protect you against any known military jet. It will get you to Florida in about an hour and a half. Top speed is nine hundred fifty miles per hour. Auto pilot is programmed to take you where you need to go. Just tell the flight computer to go, but I'd recommend having Snap navigate for you. Has all the up to date shielding against electrical attacks and brand new sidewinder countermeasures in case anyone tries to take you out in an air-to-air fight. Snap, have you been able to disable the tracking satellites?"

Snap spoke to them over Mary's device. "I have. However, there is a new problem. I intercepted a communication from the Stealth flyer. Of course, I have been monitoring all communications, but so far, they have all been heavily encrypted. This latest one had a TVCom League encryption that I am familiar with. It was a message from Theodora Devereaux to the TVCom League. She transmitted the technical specifications for the Stealth flyer to a TVCom location in Florida. I am afraid that the Stealth AV is quite a bit more advanced than any known military jet, even more than your modified Lockheed F-700."

"Oh, dear," Merryweather said. "Then you'd all best be getting on your way."

The group went back to get Deque just as he was finishing up his modifications. "I'm ready."

Austrian suddenly froze. "Theodora," he said to himself. "If she thought it was safe to send an encrypted message then she would have to be near an amplifier. Which means the vector navigation will incorporate that into its search..."

Merryweather pointed to the hanger. "Go."

As they made their way to the F-700, Snap spoke. "There has been a sudden change in the Stealth vector search pattern. The Stealth flyer is currently forty kilometers south south-east of the farm. I recommend against trying to escape on the F-700," Snap said. "Based on my analysis of the specifications sent to the TVCom League by Theodora Devereaux, I can estimate that the Stealth AV will be capable of penetrating any counter targeting cloak and will intercept and destroy the F-700 within twenty minutes of departure."

"Oh dear. This is getting tricky," Merryweather said. "Snap, would you display those Stealth Flyer specs on this screen here. Let's see what we have to work with."

Jason and Deque huddled around Merryweather's side and peered eagerly at the display. However, Merryweather flashed through the fifty screens of schematics so quickly, Deque and Jason were unable to follow along. "Well, well. I don't think I have anything here that can beat that."

"Do they know we're here?" Mary asked.

Merryweather shook his head. "No, see their sensors all use light waves and magnetic waves. Even gamma rays can't penetrate this barn."

"We can hide in here for a while," Deque said, "But they aren't going away until they've searched every last inch of this place."

Merryweather nodded. "I hope so. Because we're going to have to do this the old fashioned way."

"What do you mean by 'the old fashioned way'?" Deque asked.

Austrian answered. "There is only one way out of here. They will arrive shortly. The only way we will make it to Florida is on the Stealth AV."

"How do we do that?" Deque asked.

Austrian had a blank stare. He dipped into and out of some sort of trance.

"We are going to steal it from them."

It had been a harrowing night following one lead after another. Agent Haan was growing increasingly irrational and agitated at each juncture and it appeared that even Senator Redstone was growing frightened of her. There was a great sense of relief when they located the heavily shielded barn.

As the Stealth flyer hovered over Dr. Merryweather's farm, Agent Haan gave her tactical analysis. "There is one person in the house, an adult female. I cannot penetrate the barn, which means it is highly shielded and highly suspect. If they are here, that is likely where they are hiding. There are two automobiles in a non-shielded structure."

"Disable them," Senator Redstone said.

Agent Haan launched two electrical disrupters at each car. "They may have more sophisticated means of transportation in the barn. Before we set down, I will set the flyer to automatically fire on any vehicle leaving the barn."

"Good gravy!" Diana cried. "Warn them. They don't know what you're going to do."

The flyer landed. Agent Haan switched on the external amplifiers and said, "Occupants of the barn. Exit the building and lay face down on the grass. Any attempt to flee and we will fire."

The occupants of the flyer watched the barn intently. The barn made no reply.

"I've been scanning the surrounding area for weapons," Agent Haan said. "The shielding around the barn extends for fifty meters underground. The base of the shielding forms a semi-torus, a common base for a fusion reactor. It could be the power source for a particle weapon."

"Can they get us in here?" Theodora asked.

Haan made a curt shake of her head. "Unlikely. Though I cannot be one hundred percent certain without knowing the identity of their weapons."

"I don't want this to turn into a standoff," Carol said. "They could stay in there for months."

Agent Haan turned to the senator. "I recommend we not leave the flyer. However, in light of the fact that we are unlikely to gather any additional data or call for backup, there is a high probability that I can penetrate the structure on foot."

"Do it," Senator Redstone ordered.

Agent Haan removed a head-to-toe shiny black jumper from beneath her seat. "Good heavens, what's that?" Diana asked.

"This is a flack suit. It will protect me from attacks from energy and ballistic weapons, as well as conceal me from known surveillance methods. The suit's particular performance perimeters are classified." Agent Haan zipped on the suit and put on a helmet. She typed a code into a panel and a console opened. Agent Haan withdrew a compact laser rifle and activated its sensor screen. "In the improbable event that I am disabled, do not attempt to retrieve me. If I am not able to deal with a threat, then any of you will certainly be helpless against it. Senator Redstone has ops control of the flyer in my absence. Only her command will be able to activate its auto pilot and return you to the base." With that, Agent Haan strode from the flyer and approached the barn.

The women watched a monitor display of a camera in Agent Haan's helmet. Agent Haan stood before the barn door. Her helmet's visor revealed several external locks that were not activated. The door was as heavily shielded as the rest of the structure. But, the door swung open at her touch.

Diana knew Haan was walking into a trap, but kept quiet. Haan apparently had a very high opinion of her abilities.

The interior was pitch black, but Haan could see quite clearly through her helmet's imaging system. After several scans she could detect no people or weapons. As Diana watched, she felt some intention flowing from agent Haan-- she could sense the presence of her true quarry nearby—Austrian Tyrol. As she took another step into the barn she was about to initiate an intensive scan of the floor and walls when an insect landed on her visor. It was a common honey bee. That was very odd because the helmet's electronic field should have fried the insect instantly. A diagnostic reported the helmet was functioning properly, rather, the issue lie with the bee, which was surrounded by a quantum field that protected it from the helmet's electron emissions.

Agent Haan was apparently deliberating whether she should retreat to study the phenomenon when another bee landed on her visor. And then a dozen more. She raised her hand to brush them off when the floor opened up beneath her.

14

STANDOFF

"Weeell. I don't think she's coming back," Theodora said. She then resumed scratching the back of her hand, which she had been doing for an hour. It was now bleeding.

"I agree," Diana said. "Honest to Pete, Carol, what do you think happened to her? I mean, the kids, if they're here, they wouldn't hurt a fly!"

Carol Redstone pressed the com button. "Agent Haan? Agent Haan, come in."

"I don't know Carol," Diana said, shaking her head, "You've been doing that for an hour. She would have answered if she could."

"I need to get back to New York," Theodora said. "I have pressing business."

"We really should go back and get help, Carol. No one's talked to Mary, Jason and Deque's parents. And I have other students. What in the world are they doing without me there all day?"

"I've taken care of it," Carol said without looking at Diana.

"You keep saying that," Diana said. "But look now, you've treated us like prisoners. I don't like that, Carol. I don't like that one bit."

Carol ignored Diana. "We are not going back." Carol stood up. "I'm going out there."

"You can't do that!" Diana said. "Agent Haan said you shouldn't."

Senator Redstone smiled and said, "If I didn't know better, Diana, I'd think you were trying to use reverse psychology to get rid of me." Carol was already putting on a suit and helmet she found under her seat. "I'm not going into the barn. I'll just look in the door. It's still open."

The second Senator Redstone stepped out of the flyer, Diana took the command seat and tried to open a com channel.

Theodora frowned and took the seat beside Diana. "What are you doing?"

"I'm calling a friend of mine in Washington."

"But you can't get an outside channel in here. You have to be outside and I'm sure only Senator Redstone and that really rude FBI agent can open the door or make a call."

"I know that, but, heavens, there must be a way," Diana said.

As Diana worked at the panel, Theodora said, "I have a very good friend in Congress. I think his name is Dershel, or Robert, or something like that."

Theodora peered out the windshield as Diana fidgeted with the controls. Senator Redstone was gingerly approaching the darkened barn door. "I can see inside the barn," Redstone said, her voice coming to them over the com system. "I don't see any people. No sign of Agent Haan. I see several bees in the barn."

Suddenly a light flashed on the control panel. Diana quickly pulled her hands away. "Warning," the flyer said. "Unauthorized access attempt will result in the release of nitrous oxide."

"Seeee! You see that!" Theodora shrieked. "You better leave that alone like I told you."

Diana was gingerly holding her hands above the control panel. "Yes. I suppose you're right."

Some broken static came over the com. "I'm getting a fragmented transmission from Agent Haan," Redstone said. "She said something about falling down. She may be hurt."

"Oh, Carol, if she's hurt you have to help her," Diana said. "I mean, honestly, she'd do it for you."

Carol didn't respond, but Theodora gave Diana a questioning look. "Do you want the senator to get hurt?" she whispered. "Is that what you're up to?"

Diana made an expression of hurt shock. "Of course not! Senator Redstone and I are like sisters." *Like estranged sisters*, Diana thought to herself to make truth of her lie.

Theodora frowned in disbelief.

"Sisters do quarrel, you know," Diana said, defending herself.

They watched as the senator slowly entered the barn. "I still don't see anyone. It's possible tha--" They heard a thud followed by a metal clang.

"Carol what happened?" Diana asked. "Carol?"

"It sounds like she fell into a pit," Theodora said. "*Infierno.* That means hell. Sometimes I speak Spanish without knowing it. I spent a lot of time in South America when I was a girl. My parents sent me to private school there."

Diana raised her hands like she didn't quite know how to respond. "I uh, that's very interesting. Should we--"

"Well now that those two are out of the way we can go back to Washington. I wonder if we can get this thing to drop me off in New York?"

"Probably not," Diana said. "I can't believe this. The kids are gone, Senator Redstone is gone and that FBI woman is gone. This is just the longest trip around the fence I've ever seen."

"You call this a trip around a fence!" Theodora exclaimed. "Because the first thing I'm going to do is call the police." Theodora madly waved her hands around at the flyer. "I was kidnapped! Oh, and I guess you were too." Then Theodora smirked. "By your 'sister.'"

"Okay now," Diana said. "We have to figure out how to access this thing without Carol or Haan."

"Look at that!" Theodora said, pointing out the windshield.

An old man was walking out of the barn, toward the flyer.

"Oh my stars!" Diana cried. "It's Maxtone Merryweather! He was up for the Nobel Prize the same year as me!" Diana pressed her hand against the flyer door panel.

"The door is locked," the flyer said. "Unauthorized access attempt will result in the release of nitrous oxide."

"Well then how do we get out?" Diana asked.

"The flyer systems may only be accessed by FBI Special Agent Haan or Senator Carol Redstone," the flyer said.

"Oh, good gravy," Diana said. "Is there a water glass in here anywhere?"

"Why? Are you thirsty?" Theodora asked. "I have kept myself well hydrated to guard against dehydration."

"Oh I'm not thirsty," Diana said. "It's just these voice locks are so silly. If you give them the whole range of a person's voice they just think it's all okay."

"Well there's some glasses in that cupboard by the stinky little bathroom."

Diana fetched a glass and filled it halfway with water and returned to the door. After a minute of study, she found the pinhole microphone port. Holding the glass next to the port, Diana dipped her finger in the water and slowly ran it around the glass rim. The glass began to emit a ringing sound.

"Hmmm. E natural," Diana said. She then held her mouth level with the glass and sang a "Faaa" that matched the glass's sound. Once the sounds were in sync, Diana modulated the Fa up the musical scale, with several minor discordant notes added between the major keys. The combined singing and glass ringing created a high pitched overtone that vibrated throughout the flyer structure.

Theodora stuck her fingers in her ears.

The overtone continued to grow until it was out of the range of human hearing.

The flyer door opened.

Diana dropped the glass and ran out into the grass. "Max! Hi Max!"

Maxtone Merryweather held his arms open as Diana ran toward him and embraced him in what could have been a scene from an old romantic film.

"Where are the kids?" Diana asked.

Jason, Mary, Deque and Austrian walked out of the barn.

"Hi Dr. Saint Sommers," Mary said.

"What on Earth is going on?" Diana asked.

Theodora came running up. "Austrian. Do you have any idea what your performance appraisal is going to look like next quarter?"

"And what happened to Senator Redstone and Agent Haan?" Diana asked.

Merryweather made a calm-down motion with his hands. "They're in the barn. I've got them in a trap that probably won't hold them for long. They did trespass on my property, heavily armed, I might add, so I don't think I've broken any laws. And now these folks have to get going, so they'll need to borrow your plane."

Diana shook her head. "Go where? What's going on?"

"I don't think we have time to explain right now," Austrian said.

"Austrian!" Theodora shouted. "Have you forgotten that I'm your boss?"

"You're welcome to come with us," Austrian said, motioning to both Theodora and Diana.

"Go where?" Diana cried. "Look it, I'm as confused as a dog in a whistle factory."

A muffled blast came from the barn.

"We better get out of here," Jason said.

"Come with us, Dr. Saint Sommers," Mary said.

"Go with you where? Look now, I really need some answers."

"We have to go--" Deque covered Mary's mouth with his hand.

"We can't tell you where we're going," Deque said.

Diana shook her head. "Well I suppose it doesn't matter. Whatever you kids are doing, I just can't go along with you. I mean, heavens, I've got my other students and the program and I can't get all mixed up in something I don't know anything about. But whatever you're doing, it must be for the good because I don't think Max here would ever be involved in something bad."

Another blast came from the barn.

"Are you going to be all right, Dr. Merryweather?" Mary asked.

Merryweather pointed to his house. "In five minutes the Mrs. and I are going to take a long vacation far away from here.

A gurgling sound came from Theodora. "Hmmmph. I don't think you'll be going anywhere. That FBI woman disabled all your vehicles."

Merryweather smiled. "Oh, I think she might have missed one."

"Come one," Jason said. "Let's go."

"You won't get very far," Theodora said. "That flyer won't work for you."

"Oh, on the contrary, my dear," Dr. Merryweather said. "That flyer will work perfectly for those kids now, thanks to the specs you sent to your boss."

Theodora's jaw dropped. "That's—that's theft! The TVCom League will not stand for that!"

Diana wiped a tear from her eye. "You kids be careful."

"We will, Dr. Saint Sommers," Deque said. "You'll see."

"I know that whatever you do, I'll be proud," Diana said.

The kids each hugged Diana Saint Sommers and started towards the flyer.

Diana crouched with the kids for a private moment. She quickly caught their eyes and whispered, "I know about Dr. Merryweather's research with the bees and what happens when you combine it with my formulas. I can't stop you. Heavens only knows how you were convinced to go along with all of this. But remember--" She glanced up at Austrian, then back at the kids. "Remember, some people might say they're doing one thing, but they're really doing another."

As the children walked toward the flier with Austrian, Theodora called to him. "Hey!" Theodora shouted. "Austrian! You're staying right here with me."

Austrian turned to face Theodora. "Actually, I'm not."

"Do you want to lose your job?" Theodora threatened.

Austrian tilted his head. "That's no longer your concern."

"No longer my concern? Of course it's my concern. You work for me! And for how long now? Austrian, I can't do—I need your help with—with things, and...haven't I been good to you?" Theodora shook her head manically. "What am I going to tell Chairman Bliss? This, this betrayal of yours will be the end of me!"

Austrian raised his hands halfway, then let them drop. "I'm truly sorry." Austrian turned his back to Theodora, caught up with the kids, boarded the flyer, and they were out of sight in seconds.

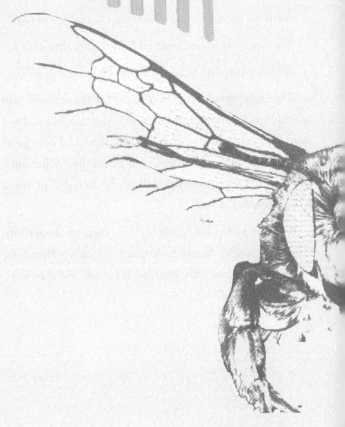

PART TWO

WINGS

15

FOUR WOMEN IN VERMONT

Senator Redstone huddled in the corner of the concrete pit as Agent Haan fired another blast at the ceiling. The barn floor remained unaffected but the shockwave caused chunks of concrete to explode off the walls, hitting the two women, their suits stiffening with each impact.

Agent Haan studied the ceiling. Deep gouges had been burned around the walls, but the barn floor above them was completely unaffected. "The floor is a carbon composite material. It is semi-resistant to all three particle beams. The carbon filaments will weaken eventually, but not before my gun loses its charge."

"There's no way out?" Redstone asked.

"Stand behind me." Agent Haan moved in front of the senator and faced the wall. Haan sent a sonar "ping" at the wall and studied her visor's readout. "These walls are six feet of concrete. Beyond that appears to be normal soil. Stand back." Agent Haan leveled her blaster.

A muffled rumble vibrated through the calm morning air.

Diana put a hand over her stomach. "Was that me?"

Another rumbled shook the ground.

"I don't think we should stand here," Theodora said. The two women hurried off towards the house.

The ground in front of the barn exploded.

Diana and Theodora turned to see several tons of soil fountain into the air. As dirt and rocks rained down, two figures crawled from the crater.

One lay on the ground, the other looked around, spotted Diana and Theodora, then removed her helmet. "Where's the flyer?" Agent Haan asked.

Diana and Theodora looked at each other. Diana didn't seem likely to give up any information, but Theodora was pointing wildly. "Her kids took it!"

"What? How could they take it?" Haan asked.

Theodora scratched the back of her hand. "Well, uh, they just did."

"Did they reveal where they were going?"

Theodora opened her mouth, but Diana grabbed her arm and whispered, "If you tell her I will let her know how they got the specs for that flyer."

"I, uh, they didn't say," Theodora said. "They uh, you know, they just came out here and off they went, just like that. It's how it all happened. One, two, three."

Agent Haan looked at her helmet, then back at Theodora. "You're lying. I have a voice analyzer in this."

Carol Redstone had pulled herself up and removed her visor. "I think you'd better tell us exactly what happened."

Theodora began to sputter. "Weell, the, uh, we just, that's—that was the truth. You know, they're very clever. They trapped you, you know."

Agent Haan leveled her gun at Theodora. "I now believe that you have been helping those kids. You will tell me everything."

"Oh, stop it," Diana said. "Sakes alive, she won't really shoot you."

Agent Haan fired a tight beam at Theodora's right leg, burning a half-inch deep laceration into her calf.

Theodora screamed.

"Oh my god! What is this?" Diana cried. "Why are you doing this?"

Agent Haan stepped closer to Theodora. "I will kill you."

Theodora whimpered. The wound in her leg was not bleeding, the laser had instantly cauterized it. Several inches of skin around the wound had blistered. "They intercepted a call I made to Jordan Bliss. He asked me for the flyer specs. Diana used her music stuff to get us out of the flyer and then the kids took it. There was a man here named Maxtone Merryweather. He and his wife took a jet out of the back of the barn and left."

Agent Haan lowered her gun. "You two are no longer to speak unless spoken to by me or the senator." She withdrew a med-pack from one of her suit pockets and tossed it at Theodora.

Diana bent down to help Theodora dress her wound. "All right now," Diana whispered. "All right. It's okay. You'll be healed up in a few minutes."

Agent Haan was listening to her helmet. She then sub-vocalized something. Haan turned to Senator Redstone. "The director wants an update."

Carol frowned. "Tell him he'll have to wait for my official report."

"He's prepared to shut down our operation if he doesn't get his update," Haan said.

Theodora's phone rang. She reached to answer it.

"Don't touch it," Haan said.

Theodora pulled her hand up to her mouth, then began scratching. "But, it'll be Jordan Bliss."

Agent Haan approached Theodora and stuck her gun in Theodora's side. "Answer it and hold it so I can hear. Then say exactly what I tell you."

Theodora nodded and answered. "Hello?"

"Theodora, it's Bliss. Did you find out what the devil is going on?"

"Uh, just a minute I need to..."

Haan murmured something in Theodora's ear.

"Uh, " Theodora stuttered. "It's the FBI. They've infiltrated our project at the TVCom League and they're planning on, on, ah—" Haan jabbed her gun into Theodora's ribs. "They're planning on sabotaging the Dunedin array."

"What! Shit. How do you know?" Bliss asked.

Theodora listened to Agent Haan, then said, "They've sent one of those flyers I was on down to Florida. It's on the way right now. It's going to fry your systems with an electrical weapon."

"Like hell," Bliss said. "Anything else?"

Agent Haan gave Theodora some more lines. "The FBI has a destroyer off the coast of South Carolina that's been monitoring the Dunedin center, operating under the, ah, old antiterrorist acts."

Bliss growled. "Just waiting to blow the beast out of us after their god-derned jet shuts us down. Well if that ain't just the bee's knees. Anything else?"

Haan shook her head. "No, that's all."

"Good work, Theodora. By the way, where the hell are you?"

Agent Haan hung up the phone, dropped it on the ground and pushed it into the soil with her boot toe.

"Shall I call the director back now?" Haan asked the senator.

Redstone made a slight nod.

Haan made the call. "The TVCom League knows about the NC off-shore. The kids used some type of unidentified technology to take our jet. Bliss probably thinks it's us heading for him. We'll need transportation."

Haan listened for a moment, then turned to Redstone. "Everything has been arranged."

16

THE TVCOM BASE

The Dunedin, Florida TVCom facility was originally the computer processing center for the television ratings company, Nielsen. When ultra-band compression made Nielsen's technology unprotectable by 2022, the company was absorbed into the TVCom League.

Over the years, the Dunedin base became increasingly important as the satellite uplink and processing base for the TVCom League, until it was almost destroyed by a terrorist group that launched five intercontinental ballistic missiles with nuclear payloads at the United States. There were five missiles, but only four targets: New York City (a prestige target), Washington, DC, (for obvious reasons), NORAD at Mt. Cheyenne in Colorado. *Two* missiles were targeted at the TVCom base in Dunedin. If destroyed, it was presumed by the terror group, not only would there be no means of civilian communication, but the spectrum space leased to everything from the world financial markets to great portions of air traffic control systems around the world would be destroyed, leaving the U.S. and much of the world in chaos for some time.

While the terrorists might have overestimated the importance of the TVCom Dunedin facility, they were not far off target. Fortunately, all the missiles were destroyed. The Star Wars defense program that was started by President Reagan in the 1980s, resurrected by President George W. Bush in 2001, was secretly completed by President Obama in 2015. The New York, Washington, Colorado and one of the Dunedin bound missiles were destroyed before reentering the atmosphere. But the surprise of having two missiles aimed at an unexpected location, the targeting system was slow in shooting down the Dunedin bound missiles. The one missile that reentered the atmosphere had its nuclear warhead blown off by a space-based rail-gun, but the missile itself, sans nose and navigation system, landed in a swamp in Everglades National Park.

After the attack, TVCom Dunedin became one of the most heavily guarded facilities in the world. Space and ground based weapons were put in place to protect the facility at all times, and a permanent military base sprouted up around it.

As the years wore on and terrorist threats decreased, the military became less willing to pay for the massive protection surrounding the privately owned TVCom League. The military pulled out most of its personnel and equipment, and the league negotiated to manage the defense system privately as long as it was still able to procure updated technology from the U.S. government. The deal was done and nothing was updated for twenty years.

Then, in 2045, Jordan Bliss became chairman of the TVCom League.

After finishing his last call with Theodora Devereaux, Jordan Bliss stormed through the massive TVCom League array master control room with Hal Rach scrambling to keep up with him. Hal had been in this room many times, but until now, he had no idea the scope of the operation.

Jordan Bliss stopped at a large control panel at the end of the room and handed the operator his executive disc. "Bring the defense systems up to full alert."

The operator, a hardened middle aged man, looked more like a captain from a submarine movie than a systems operator. He wore a jacket with his name tag: HT Westin.

HT looked at the disk, smiled, and slid it into the console.

"Why didn't I know about this?" Hal asked.

"You're a lawyer," Bliss said. "Laws are funny things. Subject to subjective interpretation."

Hal frowned. "If the government knew you had access to the missile defense system... How the hell do we still have access to the missile defense system?"

"I said I've kept us up to date. I've seen this day coming. Senator Redstone thinks she's General Washington. The government is attacking us and we have a right to bear arms."

HT pointed to a screen. "See. Nothing on radar that isn't under air traffic control. But look at this visual from the SW Satellite."

HT switched the screen display and a tiny black figure spotted from above could be seen zipping over the ground. "Passing over Long Island Sound. Three thousand two hundred sixteen miles per hour. It'll be in standard striking range in twenty minutes."

"Target five P4 missiles on that thing, Bliss commanded. "I'll bet my granny's last tooth that thing can hit us in less than twenty minutes."

A visual lock displayed on screen.

"Now find that peeping boat the FBI's got off North Carolina." While HT scanned for the FBI rig, Bliss mused and mumbled. "FBI Director Friedman, he's got Senator Redstone in his pocket. Friedman and Redstone are in cahoots, so the president doesn't know about their operation, so the military doesn't either. Director Friedman and Redstone keep the spectrum, they control all the money, making them the defacto executive and legislative leaders."

"I found the rig, sir," HT said. "They'll know by now our satellites are on them and that bird."

"Here's the tricky part," Bliss said. "Try to do this without killing anyone."

"Your orders?" HT asked.

"The off-shore needs to be taken out first. Once they're out, that jet will steer clear of us." Bliss pointed to the screen. "Bring SW satellites four and five on line."

"Activated," HT said. "But those are back-up communications satellites."

"No they're not," Bliss said. "Redirect their orbits to intercept that ship."

"Smash them into the ship?" HT asked.

"We're not murdering people today." Bliss said. "Just bring them around to a geosynchronous orbit with that ship, then I want a direct linear descent. The satellites won't hit the ship, they'll hit the water about two inches off port and starboard. They'll know what to do."

HT entered computer instructions, the satellites adjusted their orbits, fired boosters and entered Earth's atmosphere.

"They can't shoot at these," Bliss explained to Hal. "They're too small."

SW satellites four and five were indeed small. About the size of a lipstick each. They were capable of controlling massive amounts of electromagnetic energy, and were, technically, back-up communications satellites. But they could do so much more than that. The agents aboard the FBI off-shore ship had no idea what hit them. Two blinding streaks of light fell from the sky on either side of the ship as the satellites entered the atmosphere. Before they hit the water with two great seismic sizzles, they estab-lished primary communications capability for a fraction of a second, sucking a particular type of electromagnetic activity out of every molecule within a mile. The ship went dead. And the crew, unfortunately, would experience large gaps in their long-term memory for the rest of their lives.

17

A CHANGE IN PLANS

"Jordan Bliss is doing something," Austrian said. "Snap? Snap?"

"I'm on-line and searching... searching..."

Deque, Jason and Mary looked at Austrian as he squinted out the window.

"What?" Deque asked. "What are they doing?"

Austrian didn't answer. "Change our course. Don't make it look like we're heading to Florida."

"Don't look at me," Jason said. "I'm not flying this thing."

The flyer perceptibly changed course and Snap's voice came at them. "The TVCom League just dropped two of their satellites into the ocean and they have another satellite locked on us. I have primary knowledge of their military operation in Dunedin. I'm not sure their P4 missiles are accurate enough to hit us, but I've altered course."

"Agent Haan and Senator Redstone have Theodora," Austrian said. "They would have made her call Bliss and make her tell them that we were headed toward them. He thinks you kids are working for Carol Redstone."

Deque tapped a display. "Is the TVCom League going to shoot us down before we reach Cape Canaveral?"

Austrian shook his head. "What kind of trajectory do we have, Snap?"

"I've set a clear parabolic path that will take us out over Bermuda and straight into Kennedy Space Center. Jordan Bliss will realize the Dunedin array isn't our intended destination."

Jason grunted. "He's going to fire at us the second he figures out we've stolen a shuttle from Kennedy."

Austrian made some sort of "universe sniffing" motion with his head and said, "Actually, he won't."

Mary looked around. "Austrian. You're kreepin' us with the vision stuff and Deque rolls his eyes every time you say something and you know, I'm pretty easy going, but this can get tiresome."

Austrian shrugged. "You've followed me this far. You should trust me by now."

Deque squinted his eyes. "I think you pretend to be this well adjusted holier than though psuedo-spiritualist, and maybe you are, but I know all about heuristic interfaces and I can see the way organized systems work a mile away. And I can see you've got some sort of shadow self that's not entirely under your control. You don't even know about it. But if we get to the Greenleaf Space Station and you've got something else in mind besides the plan, as you presented it to us, then know that I'm watching you. I'm not letting you take over the world or any shit like that."

For the first time since their adventure began, Austrian looked angry. He spoke calmly, but there was a cold detachment in his voice that the children had never heard before. "I don't want to take over the world. I could I have done that at half your age. I want people to stop blinking out of existence. I want human beings to live and then not have to go into oblivion. I don't want to not exist one day."

The children looked at him with measured and steady eyes. Mary spoke for the group. "Austrian. We know what you want. We want it too. That's why we agreed to help. We just don't know how you make your spontaneous predictions and it makes us suspicious."

"Be suspicious all you want," Austrian said, turning his back to the kids. "My ears are open to the song of the universe. And, for all your genius, yours are not."

The stalemate ruled the flyer cabin for all of ten seconds when Snap cut in. "We will be arriving at Kennedy Space Center in ten minutes. Austrian, it would be helpful to me to know why you think Jordan Bliss will not fire on our shuttle when we try to leave orbit. Otherwise, I will have to use considerable resources to devise protective measures."

"Something will happen to separate Theodora Devereaux and Diana St Sommers from Senator Redstone and Agent Haan," Austrian said. "Our shuttle will be pursued, however. By another shuttle captained by my boss, Theodora."

Senator Carol Redstone, Diana St. Sommers, Special Agent Haan, and Theodora Devereaux stood in the beautifully warm afternoon Vermont sunshine, scanning the skies for transportation. Agent Haan said the Bureau would be sending another flyer auto piloted from Arlington. However, they had been waiting over an hour since she spoke with the director and there was no sign of a flyer.

"The Director is an exacting personage," Carol Redstone said, scowling at Agent Haan. "You lost your quarry, so now he's punishing you by putting you thirty minutes behind them. Which is a slap in my face."

Agent Haan ignored Theodora. Haan had weapons and a deadly demeanor, but Carol Redstone was an immortal in her own mind with far reaching unseen powers, so the confrontation between the two women, situated as they were in the middle of Vermont, could go either way.

Redstone continued to berate Haan. "Which means you put me thirty minutes behind the TVCom League. How do you plan on catching them?"

Agent Haan slowly opened her mouth to answer when a light appeared in the sky.

"That doesn't look like a flyer," Senator Redstone said.

Agent Haan shook her head (just once). "That is not a flyer. That is an IP-30 series interplanetary descending from a geosynchronous orbit. And it's a new version. Not more than ten years old. As good as anything the government has."

"You mean it's not from the Bureau?" Redstone asked.

"The government has never owned an IP-30. Five were built, all for private corporate use."

"So who sent it?" Redstone asked.

"I don't know," Agent Haan said, briskly striding toward the edge of the Merryweather's lawn, "but I would suggest following me several hundred meters away from where we are, as it appears the IP-30 is going to land on top of us."

The group followed Agent Haan when Diana St. Sommers gasped and pointed over the southern horizon. "Oh my heavens, look at that."

The new flyer was arriving from Arlington just as the IP-30 was descending to about one thousand feet.

"What the hell's going on?" Redstone asked, as they continued to move away from the IP-30 landing site.

A phone rang. Everyone turned to Theodora, the source of the ringing. Haan trained her gun on Theodora and said, "Wherever it's hidden, get it."

Theodora glared at Haan, then pulled a small badge out of her pocket and answered. "Hello?"

"Your main phone's not working," Jordan Bliss said, his voice coming from the badge. "That flyer with those kids is headed to Kennedy Space Center. Which means the Feds are sending them out to the Greenleaf station array to destroy our spectrum hardware."

Theodora opened her mouth, but Haan waved the business end of her gun and Theodora kept quiet. Bliss continued, "So here's The League's IP-30, landing right next to you. It would have taken another twenty minutes to get it down here, so I need you in command of it. Do you copy?"

"Yes, I hear you," Theodora answered.

"Good. Listen closely. Get the IP-30 into the same orbital plane as the Greenleaf station, lock onto any shuttles leaving from Kennedy Space Center and fire a tactical nuclear warhead at it once it's cleared the atmosphere. Got it?" Chairman Bliss asked.

"There's nuclear warhead in that?" Theodora asked.

"That's affirmative," Bliss said. "Hal says we've got enough on the legal side to justify a preemptive strike against a hostile act of the Unites States Government against the TVCom League. Those are your orders, Theodora. Follow them well, and you will find yourself in a position of high regard in the TVCom League. Copy?"

"I copy," Theodora said.

Jordan Bliss's voice came back over the badge. "Theodora, we're showing another vessel landing at your site. What's going on up there?"

Agent Haan grabbed the badge and stamped it into the ground. "Any more of those?"

Theodora shook her head.

About five hundred feet from the group, the IP-30 and the new flyer were landing, rather close to one another. The hum of their engines vibrated through the ground and made tree leaves shiver.

"Well isn't that interesting," Diana Saint Sommers said. "That big space ship's engines are making a perfect C and the lander is also making a perfect C, only one octave higher, and—this is the wonderful thing—if you listen closely, you can hear a note that is exactly in the middle. That's called a tritone. In this case the tritone is our old friend G-flat."

"We hear it," Agent Haan said. "So stop speaking."

"Oh, but I haven't got to the best part," Diana Saint Sommers said, totally undaunted. "The human brain processes this through the cochlea in the inner ear, which also controls our balance and equilibrium and such. But if the tritone is pulled in two directions, something funny happens. Like, for instance, I'll put my fingers to my ears like this and destabilize the tritone G-flat by singing the notes on either side of it, an F and G natural, like this—'ah ah ah ah ah ah ah ah ah!—it will cause severe vertigo and then you'll all pass out!"

Senator Redstone, Theodora Devereaux and Agent Haan lay out-cold at the feet of Diana Saint Sommers.

"Well doesn't that just beat all."

18

ESCAPE VELOCITY

"Which one are we taking?" Deque asked sarcastically, as the flyer landed next to three heavily guarded shuttles at Kennedy Space center.

"Shuttle Number Two, The USS Ronald Reagan," Snap answered.

Mary chewed her lips. "There's a lot of military jets flying around us."

"I have disabled their weapons and navigation systems," Snap answered. "And I am now issuing orders from The Pentagon for them to return to their bases."

As he spoke, the fighter jets broke formation and dispersed.

Nearly one hundred armed officers surrounded the flyer as Snap cut its engines.

"What about them?" Deque asked.

"Stop asking stupid questions," Jason huffed.

And with that, the flyer shot out one micro dart for each armed guard. The darts penetrated their armor, and the militia all fell to the ground, out cold. "On my signal, exit the lander and enter shuttle two's access doorway. I have overridden the codes and it will be a while before NASA is able to regain control. There will be some shooting around you, but I am implementing an ocular shifting device, so the sharp shooters will miss you by several feet. There is a two point three percent chance you will be hit by shrapnel, so be quick. Go now."

Austrian, Deque, Mary and Jason ran out of the flyer and crossed the fifty feet to the shuttle access ramp. There was some shooting in the distance, but the ocular shifting device Snap activated must have made the group appear very far away, because no bullets landed anywhere near the children.

The shuttle's interior was spacious and luxurious. It looked more like an airbus than a spacecraft. The children each took a seat and buckled their seat belts. "This is the shuttle the president takes," Snap explained.

"This is Space Force One?" Jason asked.

"No," Snap answered. "That is a decoy ship, employed for security reasons. The last two presidents have each taken The USS Ronald Reagan to the annual conference on the International Space station."

There were no visible controls. A panel in front of one seat lit up and the launch sequence was initiated and the shuttle glided about two hundred feet and lifted off. As the shuttled cleared the first puffy clouds, the floor began to swivel relative to the nose as the shuttle aimed itself straight at the sky and began its initial burn to reach escape velocity.

"It will be forty minutes to the Greenleaf Space Station," Snap said.

Jason looked at his plastic dodecahedron, with the honeybees calmly climbing around. "Well guys, we're almost there."

"I wonder where Dr. Merryweather is?" Mary asked.

"I have been unable to determine his location," Snap said. Then, "Do you have any ideas, Austrian?"

Austrian seemed to be in a trance. "What? Oh, uhm, Dr. Merryweather. I don't know."

Deque laughed. "Wow. You can't lie. That was terrible. I could see your pupils dilate and your face flushed."

Austrian ignored him and reached into his inner pocket and pulled out a small disk from his inner pocked.

"What's that?" Deque asked.

"A gift from Jordan Bliss," Austrian said.

"We are being pursued by an Interplanetary shuttle, type thirty," Snap said. "That style of ship is equipped with tactical nuclear warheads."

"Where is it?" Deque asked.

"It has just lifted off from Dr. Merryweather's farm in Vermont," Snap said. "There are four people on board. I have identified them. Special Agent Haan of the Federal Bureau of Investigation. Theodora Devereaux of the TVCom League. Senator Carol Redstone of the United States Senior Senate. Doctor Diana Saint Sommers of the United States Gifted Children Program."

"Who's in control?" Mary asked.

"I am unable to determine," Snap said.

Deque shook his head. "You better be right, Austrian."

The first thing Diana Saint Sommers did was rush into the IP-30 and get proper tranquilizers to keep her compadres from coming-to. Unconsciousness from cochlea related disorientation didn't last more than a minute. Then it took a bit of doing, but Diana Saint Sommers managed to drag Senator Redstone, Agent Haan, and Theodora Devereaux into the IP-30. Haan and Redstone were secured with hand and ankle cuffs and deposited in a small storage area that Diana imagined was meant to double as a brig if need be.

"Now how do I fly this thing?" Diana asked the cockpit.

"Voice pattern incorrect. Access denied," the cockpit answered.

"Oh, obviously," Diana said to herself. Diana looked at Theodora lying across the cockpit seat next to her. *Why do I trust this woman more than the other two? Do I trust her? I must, or else I would have locked her up with Haan and Redstone. I have perfect pitch. I could probably get her voice right before the cockpit locked me out completely.*

"Show me any shuttle launches from Kennedy Space center," Diana asked the cockpit.

The panel displayed GPS, infrared and video of the USS Ronald Reagan lifting off from Cape Canaveral. There were also several lines of government warnings about unauthorized space craft liftoff. Another panel showed more information in delayed time. Obviously the TVCom League's intelligence interception and decryption ability was quite good. This other screen showed NORAD scrambling to find ways to shoot down the stolen shuttle. SDI was off-line, ground based targeting systems were off-line.

Obviously, the kids and the TVCom AI had control of the entire US Department of Defense. "Well well," Diana said to herself. "They must be just crazy that my kids could have ballyhooed the entire U.S. national security capability." Sighing, Diana looked at Theodora. "I'll try this the right way."

Diana jabbed a hypostick into Theodora's arm and revived her.

Theodora jumped up. "Are we on the ship? Is this the ship Jordan Bliss sent for me?"

Diana nodded calmly.

Theodora looked out the window. "Where are *they?*"

"I locked them up," Diana said, motioning to the back of the craft. "We need to follow the kids,"

Theodora nodded. "Flight deck, this is Theodora Devereaux."

"Recognized," the cockpit answered.

Theodora glanced at the panel. "Dammit. They're ahead of us. Cockpit, initiate launch. Set pursuit course to follow that shuttle taking off from Kennedy Space Center, the shuttle matching... ah," Theodora looked at several displays. "These coordinates here," she said as she tapped the panel.

The ship immediately lifted off, and the farm, trees and house shrank beneath them. The new flyer sent by the FBI began to lift off and follow them.

"It must be set to some homing beacon on Agent Haan," Theodora said.

"Well it can't make it out of the atmosphere," Diana said.

"Yeah, well, I don't need it firing at us." Theodora turned to the cockpit panel. "Weapons list?"

"Atmospheric weapons will be on-line for thirty seven more seconds," the cockpit answered.

"Lock onto that black jet next to us and blow it up." Theodora said.

"Authorize type of weapon," the cockpit said.

"I don't know. Whatever you have."

The cockpit answered, "P-4 sidewinder missiles, Tomahawk G ground strike missiles, Trident 88 tactical nuclear warhead."

"Not the nuclear!" both women shouted at once.

"Just blow it up with the sidewinders," Theodora said.

"Target locked. Please confirm," the cockpit said, displaying the flyer in red cross-hairs.

"Yeeees, that's it. Launch!" Theodora shrieked.

Five rockets the size of a human blasted away from the IP-30 and detonated as they smashed into the flyer. There were five huge simultaneous explosions causing a tremendous cloud of fire. After a second, the flyer flew out of the cloud.

"Oh, good gravy. What in the name of Peter is that thing made out of?" Diana asked.

The flyer, with part of its tail missing and a chunk of wing gone, was still pursuing them.

"Fire again," Theodora told the ship.

"Sidewinder supply is zero. Select: Tomahawk G ground strike missiles, Trident 88 Tactical Nuclear warhead."

Theodora shrugged. "Fire the Tomahawk."

It was an explosion that could have destroyed a battleship. This time, the flyer was not seen again.

"Goodness. Look now we can see the curvature of the Earth." Diana pointed out the window.

"Where's that other ship?" Theodora asked, trying to match her trajectory display with what she saw out the window.

"You're not really going to fire a nuclear weapon at them," Diana said.

Theodora didn't look at her. "I have orders from Jordan Bliss. But, no. No. Of course I will not fire on them."

Diana heard the lie as Theodora's pitch shifted from her usual F to a very conspicuous A sharp. But she could not deal with Theodora at the moment. Something more serious was transpiring. The ship's decoding screen was reporting that the government had regained control of a missile silo in North Dakota and was firing a ground based nuclear warhead at The USS Ronald Reagan.

TACTICAL NUCLEAR BALLET

Snap's voice confirmed it. "The President of the United States has authenticated a launch code. The intercontinental ballistic missile has a neutron warhead. It need only be within ten miles of the USS Ronald Reagan to kill all of you."

Deque was scrambling with the Ronald Reagan's defense panel. "I'm firing everything we have at it."

Snap spoke. "Its velocity makes it unlikely to be hit by a shipboard weapon."

"Can't you stop it?" Jason asked.

"No," Snap said. "This part of the Department of Defense is an isolated system. Quite old, likely, considering the amount of time it took them to bring it on-line."

"Snap, don't you have control of SDI?" Deque asked.

"I do," Snap answered. "And I have an orbiting rail gun firing at the missile, as well as the principal ground laser canon. However, SDI hardware was only effective on rocket technology pre 2030's. It was necessary to take control of it because it could shoot down something slow like a space shuttle."

"We're leaving the atmosphere," Austrian said quietly, his arms floating momentarily before artificial inertia was established.

Mary's eyes started to turn red. She was quietly crying and looking out the window. She turned to Austrian. "Are we going to die?"

Austrian took Mary's hand. He clearly was not capable of offering her emotional support. It suddenly became clear to everyone in the cabin that Austrian had never shown emotion. It was clear then because they were kids and he was the adult. It was what he was supposed to do. But he didn't. There was something wrong. He was not able to engage outwardly. He saw their looks and realized what they thought.

"I'm sorry," Austrian said. "I am sorry that you are scared. But we won't die as long as my boss hasn't changed her morality system since we left work yesterday."

Diana Saint Sommers thought for a moment about calling the president. She knew President Mary Feinstein well enough that she just might get her call through. But that would take too long. The question was, could she control the ship if she had to? Well, there was no other way, and all she needed to do was give Theodora Devereaux a little push.

Diana watched Theodora. As the missile traced its trajectory from North America to the USS Ronal Reagan, Theodora's face fell. She was the one who was supposed to stop that ship, stop the kids, stop the government from destroying the TVCom League. Here sat a person who had spent her whole life trying to be a somebody in a huge bureaucracy, and after years of toil, she was about to break through that final layer. Instead, somebody beat her to it.

"I don't understand." Theodora said in a voice so sad Diana couldn't help but pity her. "I don't understand why the government would destroy its own ship." Theodora looked at Diana with a completely broken face.

Diana slowly slid her hand down next to her seat and palmed a hypo stick. She took a deep breath, like an opera singer before the first note, and began her lie. "Theodora. It must be a trick."

Theodora's eyes lit up. "Yes! They know I'm going to destroy the ship, so they're trying to trick me."

"Of course," Diana said. "But I thought you were *not* going to fire on that ship. On the children."

Theodora shook her head and wildly tapped the weapons console. "No. I have to. Jordan Bliss told me. The government—your students. They're brainwashed. They're not human. They're attacking us! Don't you get it?"

Diana just watched Theodora. "Target the Trident 88 Tactical Nuclear warhead on the USS Ronald Reagan and fire."

"Confirm target," the console said, displaying the USS Ronald Reagan in red cross-hairs.

"Confirmed," Theodora said.

"Authenticate strike code," the console said.

Theodora looked around. "Oh. Uhm..." Theodora accessed her mail directory from one of the console panels. There was a message from Jordan Bliss. Theodora read it. "Authorization, Bliss, alpha, gamma, gamma, omega, delta, sigma, *delta*—"

"Confirmed," the panel said. The Trident 88 nuclear warhead was released from the ship and shot off toward the USS Ronald Reagan.

"What's the time to intercept?" Theodora asked.

"Two minutes, twenty two seconds," the console answered.

"And how long until the other missile, the one from Earth intercepts the USS Ronald Reagan?" Theodora asked.

"Two minutes, thirty nine seconds," the console answered.

Theodora sighed in relief. "I did it." She looked at Diana. "I did it!"

Diana reached out to pat Theodora on the arm. "You did it," Diana said, as she stuck the hypostick sharply into Theodora's flesh.

The following thirty seconds were never to be a permanent part of Diana Saint Sommer's memory. Rage flooded her body with adrenaline, ensuring that her mind would not properly store her actions. She was looking at a woman who was going to murder four people so that she could get a promotion. She was looking at Theodora Devereaux, the woman who would murder her students. Diana was so savage with the hypostick, she felt it hit bone in Theodora's arm. She shoved the needle with violent strength, her knuckles white, and watched a shock of pain wrack Theodora's face before she lost consciousness. Diana yanked the needle out of the prostate woman's arm and lifted it again, and in the process of plunging it down, her rage cleared, her arm twitched, and the needled hit the floor and snapped.

Diana sat in her seat, looked at the panel and began a breathing exercise. She hummed the slightly off pitch F that was Theodora's vocal tone. Diana brought to mind Theodora's speech patterns, the way she could recall every note in a Brahm's symphony. It was a delicate, exact process that took time, and she was down to two minutes.

Diana breathed, and her voice became that of Theodora Devereaux. "Change Trident 88 target coordinates," Diana said.

"Enter new coordinates," the console replied, recognizing the voice of Theodora Devereaux.

Diana breathed again. One wrong note and it would be over. "Target the land based missile and detonate as soon as it is within range of explosion."

The panel mapped the new directory.

"Confirm," the panel said.

"Target confirmed," Diana said.

The console continued to respond to her. "Authenticate strike code."

Diana looked at Theodora's open mail, and read the verification sequence. "Authorization, Bliss, alpha, gamma, gamma, omega, delta, sigma, delta—"

Diana's heart skipped a beat and her blood drained from her face. "Delta" was said a sixteenth of a note too low.

Diana Saint Sommers had hit a wrong note.

And the console knew it. "Access denied."

"The IP-30 has launched a Trident 88 nuclear missile at us," Snap said.

Austrian lit up. "That's what I was waiting for." He held the small silver disk given to him by Jordan Bliss and placed it on his console. "Snap, access the TVCom League's main directory."

"Accessed," Snap confirmed.

"Log me in under the specifications in this disk," Austrian said.

There was silent activity. The panel displayed the text:

Username: Bliss Emergency 845699-LXTVG
Password: ********** (encryption retro-decay equation active)
Access: All directories

"You're in," Snap said.

"Activate TVCom League emergency user I.D.," Austrian told the console.

There was a three second delay as his command was broadcast to Earth, processed, then broadcast back up to the ship. "User ID activated," came the response

Austrian leaned forward. In twenty seconds, the IP-30 missile would be close enough to destroy the USS Ronald Reagan. "TVCom, remove Director of Affiliate Research, Theodora Devereaux, from the organizational structure."

"Theodora Devereaux is no longer employed by the TVCom League," came the delayed response.

"Access TVCom League IP-30 vessel, change Trident 88 strike target to these coordinates," Austrian said, and forwarded the trajectory of the other missile. "Forward all old mail from Theodora Devereaux's directory to Austrian Tyrol."

There was the painful delay. "Confirm new coordinates. Mail forwarded."

"Confirmed," Austrian said.

"Authenticate strike code," the console said.

Austrian opened his mail and found the message from Jordan Bliss to Theodora Devereaux. "Authorization, Bliss, alpha, gamma, gamma, omega, delta, sigma, delta."

"Confirmed," came the response. The Trident 88 changed course. Sixty miles below the USS Ronald Reagan, the Trident 88 exploded, destroying the American neutron bomb.

"What just happened?" Hal Rach asked Chairman Jordan Bliss, as they watched the nuclear missiles explode far from their target.

"I forgot about that." Chairman Bliss stood up, picked up his chair and smashed it on the floor. "This is the biggest mistake I've ever made in my entire life."

Hal shook his head. "What?"

Chairman bliss motioned to Hal's seat. "I need to sit. My chair's broken."

Hal stood and let Jordan Bliss have his chair. "I'm going to show you something. And then you're going to think of a way to cover it up. And you're going to do that because if it gets out, the TVCom board will unanimously vote me out of my job, and you'll go with me."

Jordan Bliss opened a directory and spoke. "Status, Theodora Devereaux."

The TVCom computer answered. "Unknown. Theodora Devereaux was the former Director of Affiliate Research. Her position at the TVCom League was terminated September 14, 2061, 3:49 PM Eastern DST. Termination resulted from a classified TVCom emergency, and was authorized by TVCom Chairman Jordan Bliss."

"You fired her?" Hal asked. "Right when she was firing a nuclear missile?"

"No, not me, that kid. Her assistant," Bliss said. "I gave him a chief executive corporate officer disk." Bliss shrugged. "I had an instinct. Theodora—that woman! She's nuts and incompetent. Oh, come on. You could see it. It was that assistant of her's who did all the work on Snap. He's the one who knew what he was doing. And I thought she was just using him. I figured Devereaux would get in the way at a critical moment and he'd have to take over. But all this time, he was using *her*."

"For what?" Hal asked.

"Damned if I know. And damned if anyone knows." Bliss shook his head. "No, he's been with the kids, and the government's been trying to get them just as hard as we have. They don't know what's going on either. That's why they launched their own missile from that outdated site. Snap's got control of everything."

"They're not out for a joy ride," Hal said. "Their actions have clear intent. What do they want?"

"I don't know," Bliss said. "But I know someone we need to talk to."

"Who?"

"Shut up and start erasing computer memory and depolarize backups. Let me try to keep my job long enough to make it look like I did the right thing."

DIANA AND THE
SPACE SHUTTLE

Diana Saint Sommers had never been in a space shuttle before, let alone fly one. She'd never bound people up and locked them in a closet either. After she dragged Theodora into the brig and set course for the Greenleaf Space Station, she relaxed and watched the earth's crescent glow out the window. The blinking red light on the panel would have been much easier to ignore if it wasn't accompanied by a harsh buzzing sound. Why couldn't it play a pleasant little tune instead?

Sighing, Diana pressed the button. "Hello?"

"Who's this?" a man's voice asked.

"You called me," Diana said, "Therefore, you, sir, are obliged to tell me who you are first."

"I'm Jordan Bliss."

"Oh, hello Mr. Bliss. This is Diana Saint Sommers."

"What are those kids doing?"

"If anyone knew that, do you think you'd have seen such a mess these past few minutes?" Diana asked.

"No," Bliss answered. "Where's Theodora?"

"I had to sedate her and lock her up with Carol Redstone and that dreadful FBI agent."

Chairman Bliss let out a loud hearty laugh. "You, dainty little Diana Saint Sommers, that delicate southern belle I've seen on TV, managed to drug and lock away Theodora, Senator Redstone, and an FBI agent?"

"Yes. I was able to do that."

Bliss laughed again. "Lady, you're all right. And you just might be in more trouble than me."

"I'm not trying to make trouble," Diana said very sternly. "Theodora was going to kill those kids because you told her to. And listen, mister, while I have you on the line, don't think for a minute I won't see you in prison for attempted murder. If you were here I'd lock you up too."

"I bet you would," Bliss said. "Chairmen of mega corporations come and go, and with those positions go their power, their self-identities even. But celebrity Nobel prize winners, people with their names in textbooks like you, you have more power than I ever could."

Diana tilted her head. "Honest to Pete, you're suddenly a humble rascal. Why did you call?"

"I'm exposing my belly to you. I made a mistake. I thought you were with the feds."

"I'm a teacher, and I was working on a project for the government. But it has quickly become obvious to me that Senator Redstone is involved in something very unpleasant that I want nothing to do with. And her career is also over. My last two days have not been documented. I'm sure she saw to that, so it will come down to my word over her's. And people will believe me."

"Yes they will," Bliss said. "Which is why I want to be on your side. So, can you at least guess what your kids are trying to do?"

"I can guess. In the past five minutes I've had time to think about it. I've got a pretty good idea what the kids think they're doing. It's that boy who works for you I'm not so sure about."

"Theodora's assistant?" Bliss asked. "Austrian Tyrol?"

"Yes. I think he's told the children he's doing something great for humanity. There's only one thing he could be doing with research from Dr. Merryweather. But I think he's up to something else all together."

"And you're not going to tell me a thing about it, are you?" Bliss said.

"Of course not. You tried to kill them."

"But I saved them," Bliss said. "I gave Austrian an emergency access ID. He was able to fire Theodora from the TVCom League and redirect the missile."

Diana played his last statement over in her mind. He was telling the truth. "Why did you give him that kind of power?"

"I had a hunch he'd need it," Bliss said.

"Well you were right about that," Diana said.

"Still going to put me in prison?" Bliss asked.

Diana pursed her lips. "I'll have to think about it."

"Okay, you ain't talkin'. Fine. But I'm trusting you here. Your students, and Austrian, they're up to something. Maybe they're going to do something good, maybe not. So I've got a suggestion for you. Make sure you get to Greenleaf Space Station ahead of them. You're in my IP-30, which can go faster than the USS Ronald Reagan. I made sure of that when I bought it."

"Well give me some credit. I did win a Nobel Prize," Diana said. "Check your display, Mr. Bliss. I spun up the booster. I'm showing my arrival at Greenleaf fourteen minutes ahead of the USS Ronald Reagan."

"That-a girl," Bliss said. "Now how are you going to get in? The kids control that thing."

"Mr. Bliss," Diana said, pausing as if explaining a difficult concept to a child. "The children control the United States access protocols. Greenleaf is an *international* space station."

After she hung up with Jordan Bliss, Diana called her friend.

"Good afternoon, Office of Homeland Security," a receptionist said.

"Oh, hello. This is Diana Saint Sommers. Is Secretary Wallach in?"

"I'm sorry Ms. Saint Sommers. Secretary Wallach is in a meeting. May I take a message?"

"Oh he is? Dear me. This is very important. Can you tell him that Diana Saint Sommers is calling?" Diana said.

"I'm sorry, Ms. Saint Sommers. Secretary Wallach cannot be interrupted right now."

"Oh, I understand. It must be a very important national security meeting that probably has something to do with that business about those nuclear missiles and the stolen space shuttle and the TVCom League shuttle that's following the stolen shuttle. If you could have him call me back when he's free, I'm on the TVCom League shuttle right now. If you could tell him, when he's free, that I, *Doctor* Diana Saint Sommers, was kidnapped by Senator Redstone and--"

"Please hold."

Diana waited less than twenty seconds before her old Columbia colleague, Dr. Walter Wallach, former professor of international studies, now Secretary of Homeland Security, greeted her on the other end.

"Diana?" Secretary Wallach said. "You're on the IP-30?"

"Yes, Wally. Listen, honest to Pete, it's such a long story and I only have a few minutes. Could you put Mary on the line?"

"President Feinstein?" Secretary Wallach asked.

"Yes. I'm guessing you were in the same meeting. In fact, I'm guessing she's standing right next to you."

There was a slight pause, the line went quiet, then President Mary Feinstein was on.

"Dr. Saint Sommers, this is President Feinstein."

"Madame President. We don't know each other very well, but I need to ask you a favor."

"Dr. Saint Sommers, I hope you can shed some light on what's been going on." the president said.

"I believe so. Here's what happened. The TVCom League programmed an artificial intelligence to lead the debates on spectrum ownership. They call it Snap. This Snap was able to communicate with my students and take control of various government agencies using the Saint Sommers formula. I'm pretty sure Senator Redstone is in cahoots with your FBI Director to try to marginalize your influence, so I'd check into that if I were you. She's, uhm, locked in a closet right now. But meanwhile, my students have gone off with a young man from the TVCom League, and he's friends with a physicist named, well, that doesn't matter. I think they're going to the Greenleaf Space Station to make a broadcast to Earth that will make everyone's brains change."

"Brains change?" the President asked. "Dr. Saint Sommers, the Russians aren't happy about this. And China wants to blow up the space station. We're looking at a critical military situation here."

"Well I want to help out. If you could just call Premier Gorbinov for me and--"

"Call the Russian President?" Feinstein asked incredulously. "And say what? Sorry about all the threatening actions from the U.S. today, oh and, by the way, Diana Saint Sommers wants a favor?"

"Yes, that'd be just perfect," Diana said. "I'm going to be at the space station in a few minutes and I can't dock at the American part because Snap's got control of that. And you know the Chinese, well, they're so prickly—though it is true President Lee confessed he cried at my New Years recital. But I also played the Kremlin last winter and Premier Gorbinov loves Prokofiev. We talked for hours. He did say if there was anything he could ever do for me, just ask. So if you could kindly give him a quick ring and ask if he could have his people allow me to dock at the Russian loch at Greenleaf, I think I can straighten everything out."

Diana had employed a 5/4 tempo in her speech, and no one can refuse a request stated in perfect 5/4 tempo, no matter how insane.

There was a brief pause, after which the president said, "I'll see if I can get the Premier on the phone,"

A moment later President Feinstein came back on the line. "Dr. Saint Sommers, I have Premiere Gorbinov. He is on a conference call with President Lee Kai-sheck. They would like to speak to you."

Diana smiled. "My goodness Madame president, it seems you have me on the phone with the whole world!"

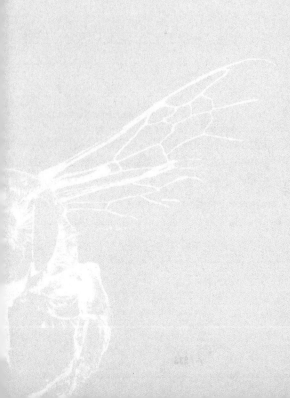

21

GREENLEAF SPACE STATION

"Is her shuttle here?" Mary Wang asked, looking out the Greenleaf loch window.

Snap answered. "The IP-30 is on the far side of the space station. I still have not been able to access the contents of Diana Saint Sommer's communications with Earth."

"You have to transpose them using the St. Sommers Formula until it makes sense," Mary said.

"I have tried," Snap answered. "Diana Saint Sommers has modulated it in a way that is making it difficult to transpose. I have tried forty million permutations of the formula."

"She knows what we're doing," Austrian said.

Mary shrugged. "Good. Then she'll help us."

"No, she won't," Austrian said.

Jason and Deque glanced at each other, then at Austrian. Their small amount of trust in him was at its breaking point.

The group moved along the air loch and passed through the primary ramp into the American entrance of the Greenleaf Space station.

"We have to go up there to get to the communications array," Jason said, looking at the schematics on his PC.

The Greenleaf Space station was basically a cube with a domed top and four docking stations. The station was primarily a communications array, unmanned except for occasional maintenance work. Soft lights came to life as the group entered the loch and found the locker of electro-static suits. The station monitored them as they put on the white suits with American flags emblazoned on the breast and each suit arm. The main doors opened and the group walked up the ramp to the main room of the communications array.

And there she was, in a bright red anti-static jumper with the blazing Tzarist Eagles of the Russian Federation--Diana Saint Sommers.

"Dr. Saint Sommers!" Mary said and ran up to Diana. But Diana didn't take her sights off Austrian Tyrol.

Austrian met Diana's stare as he slowly walked an arch around her to the center of the array. It was clear that they were locked in a silent battle. Diana stood her ground, never moving. Austrian made his way toward the array as if walking against a powerful wind, but with every step he took ground from Diana. He was younger and stronger, Diana was older and she could draw energy from unknown sources. Finally, a few feet away from the array, Austrian stopped, whether by choice or not was unclear.

"You're wasting both of our energies," Austrian said.

Diana blinked and the battle was halted. "You have us all here. You counted on me getting here, now that I know what you want to do. If Max Merryweather had any idea what you were really doing with his technology, he'd never have helped you."

"I knew it," Deque said. "You aren't going to activate the Merryweather gene sequence!"

"Yes I am. I need everyone on Earth to have access to their ancestral memories. It's critical to my work," Austrian stated plainly.

Diana stepped toward Austrian. "But what do you intend to do with all those memories, since they all lead back to you?"

Austrian's face changed slightly, some first sign of emotion, almost surprise. "You know about the museum break in. You just figured it out."

"Snap? Are you monitoring?" Diana asked.

"Yes," Snap answered over the station's PA system. "I am monitoring very intently since this mission seems to have elements I am not aware of."

Diana nodded. "I'll explain. It's true that the sequence of genes Dr. Merryweather isolated hold the encrypted memories of our ancestors. And those can be unlocked if humans are able to access the correct quantum state, an evolutionary change that will take another million years. Dr. Merryweather knew that I was against helping with his experiments once he figured out that the Saint Sommers frequencies could be calibrated by honey bees, amplified through a dodecahedron, and broadcast to unlock the gene sequence. And he seemed to agree that the psychological implications of having access to thousands of years of memories would be dangerous.

"So I assume that you used Snap's negotiations abilities to somehow convince Dr. Merryweather. Just as he convinced you, Snap, by first teaching you fairy tales and myths—Austrian primed you for sentience by planting human archetypes. Then he had you identify Mary, Jason and Deque, who all inherited musical genes from their parents. Then the quest to unlock human memories would make sense to you at that stage of your development. In that way, you imprinted on the children, as a baby mammal imprints on its mother. And in many ways, it all seems like a very noble cause you're all involved in. Bringing tangible immortality to mankind.

"Except that Austrian visited The Museum of Natural History in Washington six months ago and broke into the laboratory. He stole a genetic sample from the oldest remains of a homo sapien. And I now assume that you were able to graph the Merryweather gene sequence from that sample into your own DNA, Austrian. So the collective memories of mankind will all lead back to you. My question is, what do you intend to do with all that knowledge?"

The children looked at Austrian. Snap's voice came over the PA. "Diana Saint Sommers is correct," he said. "Austrian, you will need to answer her question to gain our continued aid."

"He wants to take over the world," Deque said. "I knew it."

Austrian tilted his head. "That's not exactly correct. My ambitions go far beyond taking over the world. I need to save this universe."

"Please explain further," Snap asked.

Austrian nodded. "Just a moment. I fear an interruption." He then placed the honeybee dodecahedron on the communications array interface and a light began to flash. "It is ready."

"Please step away from the array," Diana said. "Kids."

Deque, Jason and Mary interposed themselves between Austrian and the array.

"I will step away," Austrian said, walking out and in front of Diana.

"What is this all about?" Diana asked.

Austrian stared at them all coldly. "We are all facing extinction. You are all familiar with the many worlds theory. It states that at the quantum level, all possible outcomes to any event do occur, and branch off into other universes. I know this is no longer just a theory. Doctor Saint Sommers, you speak of humans evolving the ability to access information on the quantum level in a million years. But you are wrong. I have that ability. I can hear echoes from the other worlds. Voices. Particularly from my counterparts. And what I've learned is that some of those universes are far ahead of us technologically. And they have learned that, for any universe created from the big bang to be stable, there can only be one. Quantum states are unstable, and, like macro states, only *one* can ultimately exist.

"Since I have become aware of this, I have been competing with several billion other universes for dominance. In many of those other universes, I exist in a less than competent state. But in others, I am a thousand years advanced. And in some, I do not exist, such as in the universes where the Neanderthal australopithecine species evolved rather than homo sapiens.

"But this is the only universe in which the Diana Saint Sommers formula exists. The other Austrian Tyrols in other universes are constantly trying to gain access to my thoughts, to learn the Saint Sommers formulas. I have been successful in keeping them out. But they are getting closer. And in several universes, they are very close to collapsing all other timelines. We do not have billions of years until the end, and we do not have thousands of years. We have days."

This took a while to hit the groups. Was he crazy? Snap informed them that his story was theoretically valid. No, they believed he believed what he was saying. His intention was not to take over the world, but to save the universe.

Diana looked particularly upset. "Are you saying that we must kill nearly an infinite number of people in other universes to continue living?"

"Yes," Austrian said. "We are still subject to survival of the fittest laws."

"Kill or be killed," Jason said.

"But that should not upset you," Austrian told Diana. "In this universe, economic laws reside side by side with self preservation. In several billion years, we will be able to resurrect all beings who ever lived from all universes using the Tippler system. It will be in our best interest. It will maximize our utility. But there are other universes in which resurrection will not maximize the utility of the extraordinarily advanced beings who will live, and we will be lost forever."

Mary was clutching Diana's arm. "Austrian, what do you mean we only have days?"

"I mean just that," Austrian said. "You will not be aware of it. Our timeline will cease to exist, as will we."

"Wait a minute," Deque said. "This doesn't make any sense. If we activate the Merryweather sequence, then we'll all remember back through our family tree. So what good does it do you to have a gene sequence from an early human? All it'll do is make you remember the homo sapiens before the one you took DNA from."

Diana nodded. "Well just so, that's what I thought. But then I thought if I thought that, then Austrian certainly would have thought that. And I figured it out. While all of us exist at this end of the chain of living, all our ancestral memories will lead back to, well, some homo sapien. But Austrian will exist on both sides. He'll have the missing piece that he wants—he'll have access to a time before the many relevant universes of humans existed. He'll be able to see which branches we didn't take. He'll effectively have access to all those other timelines. And if Austrian can see the other timelines, his simple act of observation will have the power to collapse them. Austrian will kill every being in every other timeline."

Deque's eyes suddenly lit up. "It's like the Schrödinger cat thought experiment. If you put a cat in a box with a device that has a fifty-fifty chance of killing the cat, the cat is either dead or alive, but quantum physics says that until an observation is made, the cat exists in both states. The cat is dead in one timeline and alive in another."

"Well I can't accept this," Diana said. "I can't believe there isn't another way."

Snap's voice crackled to life over the PA. "I have checked Austrian's theories in every way. They appear to be valid to a ninety nine point nine nine nine percent level of confidence. I recommend you proceed with the experiment immediately. Our existence is in imminent jeopardy. And while you may have moral objections to Austrian's plan, Dr. Saint Sommers, you must consider others."

"I am considering others," Diana said. "I'm considering an almost infinite number of other lives. If the only way to collapse the timelines is to use the Saint Sommers formula to activate the Merryweather gene sequence, and if this is the only universe where I have invented the formula, then our demise is not imminent. We have time to figure out another way."

Austrian shook his head. "I'm not sure you completely understand me, Doctor. There are universes that are far more advanced than ours, and I am expending much mental energy blocking them from accessing our timeline. But I cannot prevent the physical incursion of an avatar."

"What do you mean a physical incursion?" Diana asked.

A sudden blast shook the space station. The door behind Diana Saint Sommers exploded. The smoke cleared, and standing with her powerful blasting rifle trained on Diana Saint Sommers was FBI Special Agent Haan.

"That is what I mean by a physical incursion," Austrian said. "She is not of this universe."

"That is correct," Agent Haan said. "I will now take the dodecahedron and kill you, Austrian Tyrol."

About to be killed, Austrian locked eyes with Diana Saint Sommers and said one word. "Salzburg."

With that, Agent Haan raised her blasting rifle, aimed it at Austrian and fired a mortal shot.

A moment is infinite.

That was the first instruction Diana Saint Sommers gave her students. A moment is infinite. If you listen, for example, to a note played in a moment, you will hear its subtle textures, its many overtones. That is the dissection of a moment in half, then in half again, then again, ad infinitum. A lot of time might be everlasting, but a moment was infinite. Five seconds might be longer than one, but one second of infinity equals five seconds of infinity, just as one multiplied by zero equals zero.

Diana did not have a lot of time to act. She had a moment. In that moment, Austrian would be killed. It didn't matter if he was right or wrong about anything. He would be killed, and then she, and then the children. Whether he was right or wrong. Agent Haan would kill them one way or the other. Unless he was right. If he was right, he could use the last moment of his life to save them. If he was right, he could destroy the timeline Agent Haan came from. If he was wrong, he could have enough knowledge, the knowledge of the ancients, the knowledge of contemporaries, the knowledge of Tibetan monks to control his physical body long enough to stave off death for a moment. One moment.

The blast from Agent Haan's rifle struck Austrian square in the torso. As the blast struck, in that moment of infinity, Diana Saint Sommers looked at her students. In that moment, her understanding of the Saint Sommers formulas and her thoughts merged with her student's understanding of the Saint Sommers formulas.

Jason, Mary and Deque pressed the necessary three panels on the array.

The dodecahedron activated.

Austrian fell to the floor.

As he fell, the Merryweather gene sequence in every living being was activated.

Eternity stopped time.

22

THE LIFE AND DEATH
OF AUSTRIAN TYROL

Who was Austrian Tyrol?

Austrian asked himself that question and over time he discovered many explanations, but not a singular answer. Though there was an answer. Austrian was everyone else. A creation of the universe.

He was born in a Massachusetts suburb. Father and Mother. By all accounts, the family was loving and adequately functional.

They were also very wealthy. Austrian's mother was a real estate developer, his father owned a large shipping conglomerate. They hid their wealth and led a rather downscale life. The family lived in a small three bedroom house in a neighborhood that any fast food store manager could afford. People did not know the nature of Austrian's mother and father's jobs. His mother purported to be a real estate agent. His father, the owner of a small family trucking company totaling five employees.

"Mom, why don't we buy a bigger house?" Austrian asked one day.

"It's all we can do to afford this one, honey," his mother answered.

His parents did not try to hide the fact they had much more means than they displayed. But it was not to be spoken of. Money was a taboo subject.

The mystery continued. Austrian spent years asking questions, only to be answered with non-answers. He had looked into computer access, bank accounts, cash hidden in the floorboards. There just wasn't a trace of it.

By the age of thirteen, Austrian began to believe that his parents were not real people. His mother brought him to piano lessons, his father took him to soccer practice. His mother hugged him before bed, his father told him he was the most important thing in the world to him. Austrian knew that this was how parents loved their children.

One day, in his bedroom, Austrian turned his computer on and it said hello to him, as it always did. His bedroom adjusted its temperature if he told it it was too hot or too cold. The auto tran that took him to school was always there when he expected it to be. There were no emotions behind the actions of these devices. They were programmed to perform tasks for him. There was no love in the actions of objects, only circuitry.

Humans had evolved emotions to survive. Anger to defend, love to procreate and keep a family unit intact. But now, emotions were not needed. Only programming of synapses was needed to secure their continuation.

Austrian dreamed of a large lake. He could swim underwater for as long as he liked, not having to hold his breath. Why should he? He was the lake. His computer used Jungian dream analysis to tell him what it meant. His dreams allowed him access to the collective unconscious. The stuff that all living beings were connected to. But there was something terribly wrong. He couldn't find his parents in his dreams. They were disconnected. They had evolved away from humanity. They had all the outward signs of emotion, but never truly had emotions. And they had passed their genetic defect to their child.

Austrian knew his parents would never realize they were disconnected. So why was he connected but without emotions?

And what about their wealth? What conspiracy were his parents involved with?

Austrian's epic dreams continued throughout the years. He dreamed of everything coming out of that lake. He dreamed of galaxies, spirals, space-time expansion, the nature of the universe. Austrian dreamed in the proper four dimensions: length, width, height and time. He then began to dream in 42 dimensions. Sixteen dimensions: length, anti-length, width, anti-width, height, anit-height, time, anti-time, anti-anti-length, anti-anti-width, anti-anti-height, anti-anti-time and so forth. Then he began to dream in 162 dimensions. Two-hundred and fifty six dimensions. The number of dimensions increased exponentially. Austrian's dreams gave him access beyond the boundaries of this universe. And he dreamed of himself in other universes. And that's how he found out about his parents' money.

At the end of his seventeenth year, Austrian accepted a full scholarship to Columbia University. It was 5:20am of June 2, 2055 that Austrian awoke, went downstairs and found the hidden doorway. He stood in the hallway on a four by four ceramic tile and pressed his hand against the wall. The tile descended one thousand feet into a two square mile laboratory. He walked around the premises and inspected the equipment that was now looking more and more familiar to him. DNA and RNA replicators.

Miles of fiber optics. Tanks of saline. None of it built by humans.

Austrian walked to the center of the lab, finding the remains of first machine that had began the construction more than twelve years ago. That machine built other machines. The lab built itself. Benign materials had been excavated and replicated into all the lab contents from the earth itself.

Austrian looked at a computer projection and found instantly the directory he wanted. It showed his mother's company, The Town Group Real Estate and his father's company, Dolomite Shipping, had over twelve years deposited two hundred and forty billion dollars into a numbered account. An account that Austrian had drawn on since the age of five to build this lab to accelerate his genetic evolution.

Austrian had blocked his parents' knowledge of their finances. Blocked their awareness to their daily activities. Collegues simply regarded them as eccentric in their modest lifestyle. Austrian had been the one to disconnect them. Austrian had been able to get at them in his dreams, as a small child. To understand that their genetic defect was an evolutionary jump. He understood chemically created emotions blocked the knowledge of everything. His divided conscious hid his own activities from him until now. Now he was the most evolved being in the universe. In this universe. He knew he faced dangers from other universes. Other Austrians had been at the same thing in other universes. But there was something here that they needed. Austrian's universe had something they wanted. He knew he would find it at Columbia University. This Universe was now guiding him.

Austrian looked at the saline tank he had really slept in every night for the last twelve years, nodded, deactivate the lab, and moved to New York City.

Diana Saint Sommers won the Nobel Prize during Austrian's first year at Columbia. He read her paper and realized that this was the thing the other Austrians were looking for. Now that the knowledge was in his mind, the intrusive thoughts of the other Austrians' probing grew stronger. He was literally hearing voices, being assaulted from beyond the physical universe.

When he input his symptoms into the school's medical computer: voices, visions of other worlds, belief that he was a savior, the computer diagnosed Austrian as having multiple personality disorder with a tendency towards megalomania.

Austrian was having a difficult time functioning and the stress of the incursions was truly driving him mad. If he was driven mad, he would not be able to properly process the knowledge of the Saint Sommers formulas.

Austrian began to fight back.

He sent the other Austrians a mental warning: damage me, you damage yourselves.

The assaults lessened in their intensity, and Austrian's symptoms of insanity began to subside.

Austrian then took his computer mental health report to a psychiatrist and was immediately put on drugs that subdued the apparently malfunctioning part of his brain. For a time, the other Austrians were completely locked out.

Austrian then enrolled in Diana Saint Sommer's class and made himself very small. Inuit tribes had writings explaining what one does when going before a god. You make yourself very small, they said. You make it so you can't be noticed, do what you have to do and then leave.

Thus Austrian attended Diana Saint Sommer's classes for four years, sitting there among the crowd of the lecture hall. She graded his papers over four years, looked out into the crowd. She never once knew that she had ever been in the presence of Austrian Tyrol.

Austrian's graduate studies took him into quantum physics computer theory. Diana Saint Sommers was now exclusively working on her Saint Sommers formulas musical applications with gifted children.

A request came into Austrian's department one day for a recording device that could register and record the new music Diana Saint Sommers was producing. Austrian led the team that wrote the computer program called "Salzburg," after the birth town of Mozart. The birth of genius, Salzburg was a program that guided a blue laser in the encoding techniques of capturing this new music, as well as the programming that allowed amplifiers to reproduce and broadcast the music.

Reference to Austrian Tyrol's work was mysteriously deleted on the final products delivered to Professor Saint Sommers.

It was clear to Austrian that his work at Columbia was finished. It was also clear there was only one organization in the world that could actually use the Saint Sommers formulas to their fullest extent: the TVCom League.

By the time Austrian was able to arrange an internship at the TVCom League, the mental incursions had resumed, and with the assault came the resulting information. The true nature of time had been discovered. Only one universe could exist. Austrian's was about to become extinct.

Quantum indeterminism had been proven well enough at a quantum level: for a particular state there are almost infinite future or potential realities. Quantum mechanics supplies the relative probabilities for each observable outcome, although it won't say which potential future is destined for reality. That takes a human observation. Within the observer's mind, the *possible* makes a transition to the *actual*. The future becomes a fixed past.

The missing piece was how? That had been answered in other universes, and Austrian was able to receive that knowledge: Human consciousness is directly related to quantum processes in the brain—a "time organ." The act of observation dictates nature's path.

That was all fine and well, and a nearly infinite number of universes shouldn't have posed a problem. Except that the second law of thermodynamics happens to apply to all universes.

Now that shouldn't be, because the second law of thermodynamics states that the entropy of a closed system tends to rise with time. Therefore, the disorder of a closed system will increase over time: a closed system such as a universe.

However, it just so happens that all universes are closed systems within one omniverse. As humans could evolve to observe other universe's timelines, they would collapse them. That must continue until only one reality remained.

So, the full scope of the problem was revealed to Austrian. It was truly a godlike task he was burdened with. But, as he was the most evolved part of this universe, it was his job to save himself. For he was the universe.

It was a simple job to realize that he needed to be able to make a global observation from the beginnings of consciousness in order to track down his own universe from the nearly infinite others that existed.

After a comprehensive review of literature on brain storage theories, Dr. Merryweather's research seemed the most useful. And the Saint Sommers formulas would be needed to make the Merryweather sequence active. The theft of the homo sapien DNA was easy.

What Austrian needed now was the ability to physically access a satellite to broadcast the Merryweather sequence on the Saint Sommers frequencies.

Austrian had the skill to break into all areas of the TVCom League computer, so when he discovered the programming specs for SNAP, all was answered.

There was an unfortunate accident that caused Theodora Devereaux's former assistant to become unable to speak or move. Austrian made up for his moral malfeasance by anonymously transferring a portion of his enormous fortune into the family's bank account so they could adequately care for the mysteriously diseased invalid. That would serve until such time as Austrian completed his work to save the universe and could undo the "accident."

Taking control of the programming of SNAP's database and cognitive analysis functions from Theodora Devereaux was not so easy. The woman whom Austrian went to work for was not the scatterbrain she became. Theodora was a brilliant and brash scientist-cum-corporate executive who knew exactly what she was doing. That wouldn't do if Austrian were to begin his tinkering with the SNAP program.

So, in his dreams, Austrian delved deep into the pool of humanity, located Theodora Devereaux, and robbed her of her talent. In a few days, she became a confused, unfocused mess. The change was not apparent to her. Austrian quietly took control of the SNAP programming and made the necessary changes, all the while making Theodora and everyone else believe it was Theodora's work.

As with Theodora's assistant, Austrian was aware of the morals of his actions, but was not troubled by them. He had, after all, no empathy for a single human. Humans were all part of one organism, and to save an organism, some times, some of its parts must be changed, transplanted, or killed.

As the SNAP project neared completion, news of the lawsuit between the TVCom League and the United States Federal Communications Commission was well publicized. Knowing he needed an applicable understanding of the Saint Sommers formulas that was beyond his ability, Austrian had originally planned to use his access to the collective unconscious to bend Dr. Saint Sommers to his will. He found, however, that Diana Saint Sommers was protected. She was an evolved human with a resistance to his method of tampering. Austrian next tried to access the children in the gifted student program. The useful children were also protected. It seemed that his dips into the collective unconscious had created sudden mutations among similarly evolved humans that protected them as a bacterium quickly becomes resistant to the same antibiotic.

So more conventional means were necessary. Austrian did not think that SNAP's diplomatic coercive abilities, no matter how advanced, would work on Diana Saint Sommers. The children, however, were easy targets.

They all fell into his hands nicely. A facial micro expression repeatedly directed at Chairman Bliss caused him to mistrust Theodora and hand over an executive disk to Austrian to make sure he could keep her out of the way once his travels were underway. The children, SNAP, Bliss, Merryweather—all gave Austrian what he needed.

By the time they were on the train to Vermont, Austrian knew an arch enemy from a more advanced universe had made the leap through non-space-time to his universe to stop him in the form of Agent Haan. Austrian had stayed one step ahead of her, and made it to his destination, and the children activated the dodecahedron.

Now, at the moment of his triumph, she had killed him.

But it took him three full seconds to die. The children activated the dodecahedron. And all he needed was a moment.

It was a sublime moment. Austrian experienced nearly an infinite number of lifetimes in that moment. He made his way back in time through the actions he had taken throughout his life, and he made his way forward in time through the actions the earliest humans had taken. There were branches all along the way, and with a single observation, Austrian collapsed each branch, billions at a time, until the only one left was the one with his dead body.

23

THE ACTIVATION

With the dodecahedron activated in their universe, Diana Saint Sommers, Mary, Jason and Deque suddenly had access to millions of years of memories. Diana gasped, first at the sudden killing of Austrian, then at a premonition of her own death. Without thinking, an unknown instinct took over and Diana quickly stepped back as a blast from Agent Haan's rifle shot past where she had been standing.

There were three more blasts, each at the children. No skill of Agent Haan could compete with the revived evolutionary survival instincts of any person now living in this universe. The children easily stepped out of the way of the blasts.

The space station was not so fortunate. The blasts hit the walls and now cracks were sucking the atmosphere out of the space station.

Agent Haan threw her rifle down and dove for the dodecahedron. She never made it. Whatever connected her from this universe to her native one ended, and agent Haan disappeared into a singularity.

Neither Diana nor the children had to be told they needed to get to one of the shuttles, preferably the TVCom League shuttle, since it was more robust than the American shuttle. The space station would be a vacuum in minutes. There was just one question.

"Should we take his body?" Jason asked, looking at Austrian's dead body.

Diana nodded. "We might need it."

The four of them grabbed Austrian's legs and escaped to the shuttle.

They were quiet in the shuttle. It didn't take more than five minutes for each of them to figure out what was going to happen. Below, on Earth, people were remembering. The things they were remembering made them angry. Diana became angry. Her mother's true motivations in life. Her dreams dashed, resentful of having children so young. Conversations her parents had, not meant to be heard. So many things, so many selfish acts. So many kind acts. Too much to know. It was happening to all of them. It all hit them hard and the first response to the activation of the Merryweather sequence was extreme anger.

Deque said it first. "It will be a holocaust before we land."

Mary looked up. "War? Do you have any idea what the U.S. government did to my family during World War Two?"

"He was such a fool. That's why I didn't marry him," Diana said. "I told Maxtone Merryweather," Diana said with a venomous snarl never before manifested in her life. "I told him, 'Our lives are full of things best forgotten. Demons we repress until we can overcome them, if we can overcome them.' I told him, 'You will destroy civilization.' But he thought empathy would prevail."

"There are so many good things," Jason said. "Why are they overshadowed by the bad memories?"

"Because they are new to you," Diana said. "You probably didn't like going to my class every day, but now it might be a good memory. You were probably mad at your parents for taking you out of school. But in time you forgot about that. How much time will it take for us to reconcile millions of years of fresh memories?"

"It's going to be a mess when we get back," Jason said.

A speaker on the vessel crackles a bit, then Snap's voice was with them again. "Five nuclear submarines have just set Condition One SQ in the North Pacific."

"What does that mean?" Diana asked.

"It means they are about to launch nuclear weapons," Deque answered.

"Snap," Diana asked. "Are you still enabled?"

"Yes," Snap said. "I have full access to all areas of the U.S. Government."

Diana pulled up some communications logs on her panel. "That's not going to be enough. I made calls to the White House. They made calls to Russia and China. Can you get in?"

There was a moment of hesitation. "Yes. I just interfaced with Russian and Chinese government operating systems and followed their paths to the majority of government operations in one hundred and twenty countries." There was a moment of silence. Then: "I now have total control over the entire global network."

"You must prevent war," Diana said.

Snap answered, "I have countermanded over three thousand five hundred and twenty six orders for military action among hundreds of governments."

"I want a full armament surrounding my building in Washington, D.C." Diana said. She turned to the children. "You are not children anymore. Your minds are full of revenge. You will control that, as I am. Do you understand?"

It was military. It was not a rhetorical question.

Diana opened a panel and removed some vials, sorted through them until she found what she was looking for. "We will take these," she said, handing out pills. "They will keep our heads clear."

Once this was done, Diana sighed an angry, bitter sigh, and leveled the children with a look never before seen from Diana Saint Sommers. "You understand, I control Snap. Snap controls the world. It is now our responsibility to protect the world."

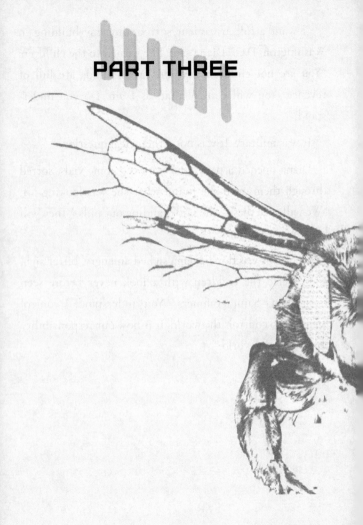

PART THREE

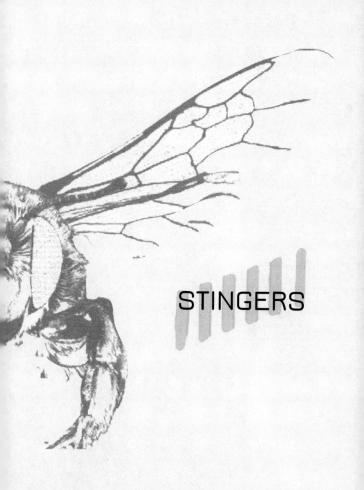

STINGERS

24

NEW WORLD ORDER

6 MONTHS LATER

"There are bees everywhere," Mary said as she walked into Diana Saint Sommer's office. "I wonder what bees eat in March?"

Diana was staring at her walls. The floating cloud scenes were long gone. Around her were real-time satellite images of the continents of Earth, with areas of wall displaying high resolution close-ups of major metropolitan areas: Beijing, New York, Mexico City, Moscow, London, Tel Aviv, Baghdad, Kyro, Washington, DC. All of them with pulsating gray clouds: bees.

Mary was about to take off her flack suit, but Diana Saint Sommers looked up at her. "Leave it on. Snap thinks there is an active nuclear submarine in the North Atlantic, here," she said, pointing to a map. "Deque and Jason won't be back for two hours and we need to send a manned flight to disable the sub."

Mary sighed. "You mean a 'girled' flight."

Mary's humor was lost on Diana. "I have a transport waiting to take you to Norfolk. Snap reports the base has completed a DSS 1 Flyer. The new flyer can withstand a nuclear explosion."

Mary turned to leave. "Wait," Diana barked. "Mary, there have been too many close calls. Force the submarine to surface, then destroy it."

It's not killing, we're all immortal now, Mary told herself, repeating the words Diana Saint Sommers had drilled into the kids as they fought several wars over the past six months. "I understand," Mary said, then turned to leave again.

"Wait," Diana called. Mary turned around and met Diana's sharp stare. "Think about the bees. Think about them. I want to see if they follow you."

"They usually do," Mary responded.

"No, no," Diana shook her head. "I want a real try. Not a swarm of bees behind you. All of them. Attempt to have the whole cloud will follow your aircraft. Concentrate!"

Mary frowned. "The cloud will shift toward me, but they can't go that fast. They can't fly as fast as a flyer."

"I know that," Diana snapped. "But I just received a request from the White House, on behalf of the Pentagon for a permit to spray some of the bees. Apparently people are afraid to go outside."

"What did you tell them?" Mary asked.

Diana smiled. "I told them that, as with everything else on this planet, we control the bees."

Mary stared are Diana blankly.

"We do control the bees." Diana insisted.

"Yes we do," Mary sighed.

"We need to show them," Diana said. "How much we control them. I want to see the cloud of bees shift and try to keep up with you."

"Yes, Doctor Saint Sommers," Mary responded, using Diana Saint Sommers formal title, which usually got through to her these days.

Diana glanced from a map back to Mary. "You should get going."

Mary briskly walked out and Diana went back to staring at the walls.

"Inform the White House that their request regarding the bees is denied," Diana spoke to the room. The message would be conveyed to the appropriate personnel at the Executive office.

"Dr. Saint Sommers, this is Snap." The voice seemed to come from everywhere.

"What is it, Snap?" Diana asked.

"It is not necessary to destroy that submarine. I have the launch codes and it is being actively monitored. I only brought it to your attention as part of daily advice."

"Still, it's a loose threat. Better to destroy it," Diana said coldly.

In the six months since the activation of the dodecahedron, hundreds of lifetimes of memories changed everything on Earth. The dead lived again. The long dead and mostly forgotten, until now. It was not just memories, a large database being brought back on-line, but personalities, people. Some were angry, some were peaceful, some were still bent on revenge, some on world peace. The initial danger was the people in charge of militaries with old axes to grind. Diana quickly killed them all. It would take years until humans adjusted, and there wasn't time to allow the most dangerous to acclimate. There were also some of the foremost thinkers of times past, with work still to be done. Diana isolated those groups and gave them resources and protection. Great advances were made in science, technology, art, music as the memories of Einstein, Hawking, Tippler, Mozart, and thousands of others lived again.

Naturally, governments were not happy to have their militaries usurped by Diana and her computer. But then Diana was surprised just how little resistance there had been. People were smarter now, and they could hardly argue the world was safer under her unifying control. The threats were too great.

The responsibility of ruling the world and the weight of so many resurrected memories killed Diana. The happy person that was Diana Saint Sommers was lost in a sea of people, disheartened by the history of her ancestors' petty thoughts and selfish deeds.

"Are there any new treatments?" Diana asked, the smallest sign of hope in her otherwise emotionless voice.

"Jelco Corp announced today a new treatment that slows rapid memory linkage in people with laddering disorders. It should help with people more susceptible to traumatized personalities. Worldwide distribution should be complete by the end of the week."

"Jelco Corp?" Diana asked. "Isn't that where we sent Max Merryweather's son?"

"Yes," Snap replied.

Diana stood and paced. She was thinking about the day at Maxtone Merryweather's farm with Senator Redstone, Theodora Devereaux, and "Agent Haan." Max Merryweather and his wife had taken a small plane from the farm shortly after Diana launched the space shuttle. Merryweather's plane exploded, and Diana was sure it was the work of Haan.

Merryweather's death was a great loss. But his son, a financial executive, was now every bit as smart and knowledgeable as his father. And employed in helping humanity survive the immortality his father unleashed.

"Dr. Saint Sommers?" Snap asked.

That was odd. Snap never summoned ones attention before speaking, which sure got Diana's attention. "Yes Snap?"

"I believe you should grant the permits to spray the bees."

This was the second time Snap had made a recommendation counter to what Diana suggested. First the nuclear submarine, then the bees. How odd.

"Why, Snap?" Diana asked. "Why do you want to kill the bees?"

"I do not want. They pose a threat to the planet's ecosystem," Snap said.

That was extremely odd. Diana played back Snap's message in her mind. It was off. Not the wrong note, not the wrong tempo, but something about it was off. Was Snap capable of lying? And if so, for what reason? It might be for protection, but Diana could not recall a time when Snap had not been forthright.

"Well that's the strange thing, Snap," Diana said. "We *thought* the bees would be a danger to the ecosystem when they first started appearing in great numbers, but they do not appear to be consuming pollen, building hives, or consuming any resources. And even the big clouds don't appear to block a significant amount of sunlight. It's like they are going out of their way to not impact the eco system. I ran all the tests myself."

"I believe your tests were initially correct," Snap said. "But I have been monitoring the bee clouds and they appear to be producing a large amount of carbon dioxide and there is now a significant blockage of sun to be of concern."

Diana looked at a display with a download of current data on the bees, courtesy of Snap. The data confirmed what Snap had reported.

Diana clicked an icon and called Mary. "Mary, are the bees following you?"

There was a moment of static, then Mary answered. "No, they aren't," Mary said. "I concentrated but there was no response in their vector." Mary showed Diana a display of the first minutes of her flight to Norfolk. There was no significant movement from the Washington, D.C, bee cloud.

Without turning her head, Diana glanced as far to her side as possible, managing to take in a partial view of the outdoors. It could be her imagination, but the bee cloud seemed to have changed slightly in density, as if they had dispersed somewhat.

"Snap, why did you bring the nuclear submarine to my attention if you did not intend to have me authorize its destruction?"

"It was inaccurately classified as a manned Subula class China Republican submarine. It is, however, a Ku class China Republican submarine, and therefore not manned. There is no chance of launch codes being compromised."

That made sense though Diana did not recall Snap ever being inaccurate.

Something was wrong.

"Mary," Diana said.

"Yes, Dr. Saint Sommers?"

"Snap recommends that we not destroy the submarine after all," Diana said. "It is unmanned, and as such it seems to me an easy decision to sink it. What do you think?"

"I agree with Snap," Mary said.

That was not the answer Diana expected. Mary would have recommended destroying the submarine upon finding out there was no one on board.

"Then return," Diana said.

Diana stood up and walked to the window.

The bees had certainly moved more than usual. And Diana did not detect Mary lying. In which case, that was not Mary who Diana was just talking to. It was Snap.

There was something wrong with Snap.

That was very bad, because Snap heard everything, saw everything, controlled everything.

Controlled everything except the bees.

25

THEODORA STRIKES

Three hours passed. Mary did not return. Jason and Deque did not return. They did not answer any calls.

Diana manually called up the flight paths of the children's flyers. The data was incomplete.

Snap's voice came over a speaker. "Dr. Saint Sommers, is there something with which you need assistance?"

"Yes, Snap," Diana said. "Where are the children's flyers?"

A moment passed, then the fliers' flight paths appeared on a screen. Snap highlighted the paths. "As you can see, Jason and Deque are currently passing over Western Africa. Their estimated time of arrival at Edwards is one hour fifty minutes. Mary's flyer has returned to Norfolk from the North Atlantic at the indicated coordinates."

Diana did not believe a word of it. But how could Snap be lying? The algorithms that governed Snap's program had no subroutines that would allow for deception. The Snap program was not a malicious intelligence. In its months of existence, Snap functioned as any computer program would – to serve the logic of its programming. The programming written by its creator. Austrian Tyrol.

Would his death have resulted in a change in Snap's intention? It was created to execute the dodecahedron program. In all logic, Snap's primary goal was ongoing. The dodecahedron program was "running" currently in all humans. Austrian's death would not change that. In Austrian's absence, the Snap program ran on the systems controlled by Diana and the children. There was no place left in the world where Snap could run outside of the Saint Sommers systems.

Diana went to a panel and called a number.

"What do you want?" came the answer of an angry woman.

"Senator Redstone," Diana said. "What are you doing?"

"Very little, Doctor." The senator replied. "Lockdown in the congressional East Wing is imprisonment, no matter what you call it."

Diana cut the connection. Senator Redstone was the same. She was the only person in the government with enough knowledge of Snap to possibly impact its program.

Diana rubbed her head and looked up at the time. 5:30AM? Was it already that late? She'd been up all night.

She checked her watch. The hands read 4:30.

"Snap," Diana asked. "Why does this screen say 5:30?"

Snap replied, "That is the current time. At 2:00AM, the computers automatically reset to Daylight Savings Time."

Computers reset.

A thought occurred to Diana.

"Snap," Diana said. "Could you please deactivate the security locks on the corridor entrance. I want to return to my room."

"Certainly," Snap replied.

Diana walked out of her office and through the main room of the former spectrum lab of the gifted children's program. She approached the hall exit and pulled on the door handle.

It was locked.

Snap had not unlocked it.

How long had she been talking to a fake Snap voice interface? Very likely since 2:00 in the morning, when daylight savings time began.

Someone else had control of Snap. Someone who would have had very specific knowledge of the Snap program to know that a code could be inserted when the chronometric program reset in October and March.

Someone who was extremely intelligent before her mind was destroyed by Austrian Tyrol.

A voice came from a speaker. A shrill southern female voice. "I am enjoying watching the expression on your face as this all dawns on you."

Theodora Devereaux.

Diana stood silently by the heavily armored entrance to the Gifted Students offices. She didn't bother to try opening the door. Her highly secured command center was now a prison.

Theodora Devereaux. "Obviously I cannot have you wondering around, Doctor. This is purely practical. It has nothing to do with the way you so unceremoniously turned me over to the TVCom League regulatory commission."

"What have you done with the children?" Diana asked.

"The children are being very helpful," Theodora said. "They don't want to see you get hurt."

"They're with you?" Diana asked.

"Of course," Theodora snapped. "You have that bunker of yours so heavily armed I don't suppose it would take half a word to Snap to blow that place clear off the planet."

"You can't possibly have control of Snap," Diana said.

Theodora huffed. "Why not? Because I'm not a Nobel prize winner like you? Because no one but you could possibly understand the St. Sommers formula? Is that it?"

"What are your intentions? What is it that you want?"

"Do you really think that you could just take control of the world and people would stand for that?" Theodora snarled. "What makes you think you are above everyone else?"

"What is it that you want?" Diana repeated.

"I want what I have worked for my entire life. But then you don't really understand anything as low as work. As toil. Everything's just come your way, hasn't it? I think people like you exist simply to make others think they are less complete, not talented, not as smart, so that you can bask in your own imagined glory."

"I'm in no mood to argue," Diana said rather quietly. "You and Chairman Bliss have taken on a great responsibility. What you do with it had better be for good and not your own personal advancement or it will not last."

"For your information," Theodora said, "Jordan Bliss is no longer Chairman of the TVCom League. That was my fist act as Acting Chair, after I assumed control of the Snap program this morning."

"And what did you do with Jordan Bliss?" Diana asked.

"That is not your concern," Theodora replied.

An image of Jordan Bliss came to Diana's mind. Theodora had been turned over to the TVCom League regulators. Their critical technology had been deactivated by Snap. After that, who knew what went on. It was assumed they were not a threat. Theodora's mind was restored, the damage imposed by the living Austrian Tyrol erased. Her mind now enhanced by the dodecahedron program, she would have been able to figure a way in. Who would have thought her ambitions remained when the world had changed? Chairman Bliss would have seen this coming. He was not a man to leave anything to chance. What did she want?

Diana knew she couldn't stay there much longer. Her life was in danger. "So, Theodora, my guess is that you were not able to hold on to Chairman Bliss?"

"He is not the Chairman!" Theodora snarled. "I am. And his flight is fruitless. His resources are almost exhausted. And I have one nuclear submarine under my control, aimed right down the throat of your little town. The debates will go on. The TVCom League will not only take its rightful place as governing body of all communications, but will also take its rightful place as the only legitimate government in this new world we have created." Theodora paused for dramatic effect. "After all, wouldn't you agree, that is what Jordan Bliss would have wanted?"

"I agree," Diana agreed. "That sounds like what Chairman Bliss would have wanted."

"He is not the Chairman," Theodora calmly said. "Why do you continue to goad me when I am about to have you taken into custody?"

Diana began to nonchalantly back away from the door.

"I know about the explosives in the door," Theodora said. "You had Deque install them, and Snap was watching. The detonator is on the third spectrum interface on the opposite wall. It is no longer active."

Three heavily armored and heavily armed men jogged down the hall and came to a stop outside the door. There was a series of clicks and a hum as the electromagnetic seal of the door released.

Diana stood quietly as the three men entered. Two held either arm behind Diana. The third man stood guard behind them and said, "We have her in custody."

"Do not let her go," Theodora commanded.

"Yes, Sir," the man responded.

Diana looked separately at the two men on either side of her. "This is really not needed," she said as they led her through the doorway. "I'm just an old woman," she said in a plaintiff ¾ tempo.

The two men hesitated and looked at her.

"Hold her!" Theodora screeched.

But in that slight moment of hesitation, Diana collapsed on the other side of the door, reached up and turned the handle in a quick sequence.

The back of the door exploded and the three men were blown through the building wall.

Alarms blared. Debris and dust fell. Diana stood and looked out the back wall. The sequence detonator in the door handle had been her own work. Her backup. Apparently Snap didn't see everything. The blast had hit the men full on and turned them into projectiles. Their armored clothes made them human cannonballs. Diana wasted no time climbing through gaping holes in the concrete wall.

Once outside, Diana ran.

As Diana ran down the path to the main entry road, she knew she was being tracked--showing up as a glowing figure on every display in Theodora Devereaux's TVCom command center. How many mercenaries had Theodora sent? Three had made it into the building to take custody of her. They would only take orders from Snap, but the elite army unit that guarded the Gifted Students compound knew Diana. At least the officers did. If she could get to the Captain of the Guards, if she could contact General Peres, then she might survive.

Bees were swarming around Diana. Their hum was loud. B flat. B flat with so many overtones Diana was momentarily stunned by the sound's beauty.

The bees were getting thicker, making it difficult to run. She didn't want to swat at them. The hum filled her mind. She thought about their pitch. Thought a pitch that was outside the range of human hearing. It was terribly distracting, all consuming, but she couldn't help it. Like a tune stuck in the mind, she thought the pitch and the bees grew thicker.

"Stop," a voice shouted. "Stop, Dr. Saint Sommers."

She recognized the voice. Looking up, she saw a uniformed man standing by the main entry road. It was Captain Jung. She knew him.

Diana stopped, panting, bees swarming everywhere. "Captain," she gasped.

"Just stay there for a minute, Dr. Saint Sommers," Captain Jung said, "Until we find out what's going on."

Gasping for air, Diana rested her hands on her knees to catch her breath, and nodded at the captain. She caught a glimpse of something in his eye. A visual nod at something behind her.

Diana jerked around and saw a guard with a stun rifle aimed at her.

The second she saw it, the rifle discharged. She could barely make out the blast glow through the cloud of bees. The bee swarm suddenly swirled into a mass between her and the blast. It was absorbed and dispersed. The blast never reached her. And it didn't kill a single bee.

Captain Jung lunged for Diana, but a figure behind him swung, hit him in the side of the head and he fell to the ground.

Diana looked up and saw an older man's sturdy figure holding a metal pipe. He peered at her through the bees, waving a hand in front of his eyes. He stepped forward, pipe clutched in his fist. She could make out his face. It was Jordan Bliss. "I'd say we better get into the car," Bliss said. With that, he grabbed Diana and they plunged though the open door of Bliss's shiny black Lockheed Hummer.

26

SALZBURG PUZZLE

Four hardened ammunition rounds hit the back of the LockHum as it barreled over a median and began speeding along Maryland Avenue. Automatic lock-down straps had pinned Diana and Jordan Bliss to the seat.

"So, where to?" Bliss asked.

Diana, shaking, put her hands to her head. "Get us out of this city alive."

Bliss tapped the instructions into a panel.

Diana looked up.

"They can't track us," Bliss said. "They wouldn't even know what this thing is made of."

"Well someone knows" Diana said. "And it won't take them long to track down that memory. Besides, there are cameras everywhere. We might be invisible to tracking, but we're not invisible."

Bliss huffed, "Worry about that later."

"What happened?" Diana asked, "To you? Why did you come get me?"

"Short story," Bliss said. "Theodora got her mind back. Got her anger worked up. Got into some uplink and got control of Snap. She made a lot of that thing, don't forget. I barely got out of there alive and used up about six lives. Not ten minutes after I got away she found the isolated TVCom system I was running on, fixed my location and shot me down over the Potomac. Had my Hummer on board. Drove up out of that swamp and over here to get you." Bliss paused. Then added, "Damn. That was my super secret system."

"What is she doing? I don't understand why you came here?" Diana asked, grabbing the armrest as the Hummer bounced.

"She's gonna kill me. She's gonna kill you. Figured I better get you and maybe we could figure out a way to not get killed."

"Well won't that be a trick," Diana said. "Did you see the kids before you left? Jason, Mary. Deque?"

Bliss nodded. "She got them. They're on synaptic interface. I don't think they're going to be much help. You know Theodora knows she'd be outsmarted by the three of them."

Diana sighed. "Well she won't kill them. She needs their minds." Diana gasped and put her hand to her head.

"What's wrong?" Bliss asked.

A piercing B flat seared through Diana's brain, momentarily blinding her. "Damn," Diana said. "The bees. They're... the sound they make. It's stuck in my head."

"What's that all about?" Bliss asked.

Diana closed her eyes to steel herself against the pain.

The Hummer suddenly slowed. Bliss checked a display and looked out the front window. "Not good," he said.

Diana looked up, squinted to see through the pain.

A Stealth AV was hovering in front of them.

"Son of a bitch," Bliss said, pounding his panel. Bliss launched a countermeasure from the Hummer just as the stealth launched a missile. The missile hit the countermeasure fifty feet from the Hummer. The blast nearly rolled the vehicle.

"I don't have many more of those," Bliss said.

Diana winced in pain, then sank back into her seat, suddenly limp.

A second missile blasted into a countermeasure less than ten feet from the Hummer. A large piece of shrapnel hit the side window with the speed of a bullet. The sound was deafening, and a spider web of cracks spread through the glass.

Diana was making a humming noise. Bliss launched the last countermeasure. It spat on its rockets above the Hummer for several moments before expiring. They were now defenseless as the Flyer was about to blow them clear off I95.

But the blast never came.

"What the hell?" Bliss asked, looking out the front window.

Diana opened her eyes.

The Stealth Flyer was covered three feet thick in bees. And more were piling on. Thick clouds of bees descended and attached themselves to the Stealth.

The Hummer took off.

Behind them, the Stealth was overcome by bees, lost control and crashed onto the highway.

Bliss let out a whistle. "You do that?" he asked.

Diana nodded.

"Can you do that again?" Bliss asked.

"I imagine," Diana said. "Can you please not speak? Sound is extremely painful to me right now."

They sat quietly for several moments as they sped along I95.

Suddenly Diana's eyes sprung open. "Theodora didn't make Snap. *He* made Snap," she said quietly to herself. "No, he *is* Snap."

"Who?" Bliss asked.

"Austrian," Diana said.

"He's dead," Bliss replied.

"Salzburg," Diana said.

"You want to go to Salzburg?" Bliss asked.

Diana shook her head. "Is there a link out on this?"

Bliss frowned, as if to say the question was insulting. He tapped a screen next to her.

Diana sped through several directories and came to the Columbia University Archives, where she called up the detail of the Salzburg program.

And there it was. A code. Diana understood the code. It was a message from beyond the grave. A message from Austrian Tyrol.

"We have to go to Westbridge, Massachusetts," Diana said.

Bliss shrugged. "No problem. So long as you can take out any more obstacles like Stealth Flyers."

"That will not be a problem," Diana said. "Theodora will not be able to track us right now."

"What'd you do now?" Bliss asked.

Diana nodded out the window.

Bliss looked outside. It was dark.

A cloud of bees blanketed the sky for as far as the eye could see.

A woman in her mid sixties stood in the doorway of a home in rural Massachusetts. She observed the sky growing darker, as if a storm was approaching. She wasn't looking at storm clouds.

The woman was looking at a cloud of bees.

She turned to her husband. "Do they show up on the weather radar, Danny?"

The man nodded. "It looks the same as if a warm front were advancing from the south."

"It has to do with Austrian," the woman said.

Danny frowned. "Our son is dead, Penny." He stood up from the table, stood by his wife and looked out the window. "I don't know what he got mixed up in. He always knew exactly what he was doing, so don't go all sad. He did something to us a long time ago. Something terrible. I know how my great great grandfather felt when the cat died, but I can barely remember the past twenty years."

"I knew he wasn't a good person!" Penny snapped at Danny. "And he would have killed us if he needed to. So don't think I'm going all sad. But this stuff about him saving the universe... Danny, you know my dreams are not just phantom thoughts. Austrian died and he's stuck in some horrible place. The universe created him, gave him powers to save it, but he had no guide. He had no idea the danger of the powers he used. Who would chose his path if they knew the price?"

"He made us remember everything," Danny said. He turned to his wife. "He did this to everyone. He brought incredible changes to humanity. Made it something it should never have been. That's what our son did. Better that he let us all die. Will our suffering follow us after death as well?"

"Oh Danny! We always knew something wasn't right. Why couldn't we break out of that numbness? Maybe we could have helped him."

Danny closed his eyes and shook his head.

Penny peered at the sky, fixed on something. "Danny. What's that?"

An object resembling a small plane appeared at the edge of the bee cloud. It was falling fast.

Penny opened the door and went out, followed by her husband. "Look. The bees are sticking to it."

As they watched, the object plummeted toward them, faster and faster as dark clumps of bees swarmed around it. Suddenly it started raining dead bees.

"Get inside!" Danny yelled.

The two slid the glass door shut as the air turned dark with falling bees. There was an incredible roar and the sound grew louder and louder, as if they were standing behind gigantic jet engines. Bees were pouring against the glass door. The roar grew deafening. Then, the falling object tore through the rain of bees and slammed into the ground with a shockwave that blasted through the house, shattering windows and jolting the building off its foundation.

Outside, in the back yard of the home Austrian Tyrol grew up in, a satellite lie smoldering in a fifty foot wide crater, covered in bees.

As the LockHum sped at 150 miles per hour up I-95, Diana was scrolling furiously though lines of code on a screen.

"What is this Salzburg program?" Bliss asked as he took a pull off a decanter filled with Kentucky bourbon. "Sounds like some artsy shit."

"It's the name they gave to the Saint Summers recording formulas at Columbia," Diana responded. She continued to look through the code then stopped as she came upon something surprising. "Well heaven loves children! Would you look at this!"

Jordan Bliss belched bourbon under his breath. "What's you got there, Sweetheart?"

Diana shook her head. "Austrian Tyrol was in my class at Columbia for years! And he was on the team that wrote the Salzburg program, but I'm looking through the code appendix and I can see he had his name deleted from all the credits."

Bliss was holding the decanter and looking worriedly at the sky. "So what does that mean?"

"Good gravy, I don't know." Diana sat back and crossed her arms. "But he's been in on this a lot longer than we imagined." Diana looked at the screen and started scanning more lines of code.

After a few minutes Diana looked over at Jordan Bliss. "Oh, listen, I'm going to need a favor from you."

"Yeah, what's that?"

"When we left Greenleaf space station I put Austrian Tyrol's body in a pod and ejected him from the TVCom League's shuttle. He's orbiting at these coordinates."

Bliss waved a hand at her screen. "What the hell do I care?"

"Oh for pity sake! Stop being such a pill," Diana scolded. "I need you to get that body!"

"In case you forgot, that loon Theodora is in charge of all things TVCom and I ain't got nothin' left she can't control except this here Hummer."

Diana looked totally exasperated. "Do I have to do everything? That was your personal escape pod, if I am not mistaken. So I'll bet dollars to date-nuts you can figure out a way to get that out of orbit."

Bliss thought for a moment, huffed, then turned to a screen. After he worked for a bit, he threw himself back in frustration, then thought a bit more and said to Diana, "Okay, I can get it out of orbit but when it re-enters it's going to land in a five-mile radius of the target coordinates and Theodora is going to be on it faster than a Chinaman on a Euro-bond."

"Okay," Diana said. "Do it. Set target coordinates to this address." Diana showed him. "Maybe I can get the bees to help us be a little more accurate."

Thirty minutes later Diana Saint Sommers and Jordan Bliss pulled into the driveway of 135 Lake Shore Drive, West-bridge Massachusetts, childhood home of Austrian Tyrol.

Two people stood at the edge of a smoking crater.

"Shit," Bliss said. "Now we got Ma and Pa all upset."

"Just let me handle this, Jordan," Diana said. But before she could open her door Bliss was out of the Hummer barreling toward the crater.

"Afternoon," he bellowed to Penny and Danny Tyrol. "Nothin' to see here. Step back this is official TVCom business. Had a little problem with a satellite."

As Diana hurried to the edge of the crater, the Tyrols looked at them in astonishment.

"Oh, dear," Diana said. "I know this is a bit of a shock. What you must be thinking! Well, let me just say--" The roar of engines filled the air and a wind slammed them. A helicopter was approaching over the trees. Then, several sirens pealed as a fleet of police cars screeched to a stop around the house.

Diana looked at Jordan Bliss. "I'm afraid we're going to have to hurry."

"Indeed," Bliss said. "You handle the Feds, I'll get the kid."

Diana nodded, closed her eyes and concentrated. A dome of bees began to form between them and the cars and helicopter.

"Hurry," Diana said, locked stiff in concentration.

Bliss slid down into the crater. "Listen folks," he yelled to the Tyrols. "Come on down here I'm gonna need a hand."

The Tyrol's entered the crater. Danny yelled, "Who are you and what is this?"

Bliss covered his hand with his sleeve and tapped a code into the steaming hot door.

"Uh, you might want to brace yourselves. This is gonna be a bit of shocker..."

The pod door slid open.

Inside lay the dead body of Austrian Tyrol.

Penny gasped. "Oh my God, Danny. It's Austrian."

"Little help getting him inside?" Bliss asked.

The parents stood frozen, looking at the perfectly preserved body of their son. He lay in the pod, face frozen in death, a charred blast mark on the center of his chest.

A noise shook them from their shock: a high pitched humming. It was coming from Diana as she created an ever thicker dome of bees.

"She ain't gonna be able to keep this up much longer," Bliss said. "So if you don't want to end up like him, I suggest you give me a hand."

Moments later they were inside the Tyrol's kitchen. Both Diana and Bliss looking haggard from their flight and the various attempts on their lives. The Tyrol's were shaking with fear at this shocking turn of events. Their dead son had fallen from space into their back yard.

A fleet of military vehicles surrounding their house, held at bay by a wall of bees. And these two strangers who had all the answers.

"I need a window," Diana snapped.

Danny touched the kitchen table. Diana went over and scrolled through the house operating systems.

"I can't find it," she said.

"What are you looking for?" Penny asked. "I don't know what you are doing but I feel we should be helping you."

Diana tapped the window. "Austrian. How did he do all this? He planted himself, he got into people's minds. He held off an incursion from other planes. He created an artificial intelligence that took control of the world and everyone's minds alive and dead. He knew this day would come. So he must have made provisions."

Bliss nodded. "I made provisions once. Let me look..." Bliss looked at the window and scrolled through some directories. "This house is 2020?"

Danny nodded.

"So no terror threat shelter?"

"No," Danny said.

"That's just the way I would have made it look," Bliss said. And with a few taps on the table top, he found a directory for sub-level climate control. "There you go." Bliss motioned to Diana.

Diana looked at the directory. She tried studying the sub-directories but she appeared not to be able to focus. Her vision was growing blurred. "I need help, Jordan." Diana slowly sat at the table. "I can't keep the bees... I can't..."

Jordan Bliss patted Diana's shoulder. "Well don't worry there little miss. Whatever's down there can generate a lot of power." Bliss started moving his way through the home's climate control directories.

"He would have known we'd be under attack," Diana said. "He would have thought of..." Diana wobbled and nearly fell off her chair.

Penny went to Diana's side and protectively held her shoulders.

Danny was looking out the window. "Whatever you're looking for you better find soon." Outside, the bees began falling like sheets of sleet as clouds of poison were launched from the military units.

"They're going to blow this house up in about one minute," Danny said.

Bliss grunted and nodded. "I am working as fast as I can." Getting nowhere with the interface, Jordan stepped back from the table and ran a hand over his face. "We always put our TVCom weapons in the climate control directory. I can't find anything here." He thought for a moment.

A sizzling series of bright lights flashed through the window. A volley of rockets hit the second story of the house. The house shook, flaming debris fell everywhere.

"We have to get out of here," Danny said.

Bliss shook his head. "We get killed either way." It was getting very warm very quickly.

"Where are the sensors for the climate system?" Bliss asked.

Danny waved his hand at the walls. "They're all around. Mid-wall every four feet. That's building code."

Jordan Bliss thought a moment. "Are there any inside rooms?"

"Only the hall by the stairs."

Bliss motioned toward the center of the house. "Let's get in there."

Penny helped Diana stand while Bliss and Danny moved Austrian's body to a corridor by the stairs. As they placed

Austrian's body on one of the hallway's four foot by four foot ceramic tiles, a small light quickly swept across the floor and across Austrian's body.

"What was that?" Diana asked.

"A signature verifier," Jordan answered. "And I think it got it."

The tile Austrian's body was resting on began to descend.

"Everyone on," Bliss said.

As they crowded onto the tile and began the one thousand foot decent, above them, the house was completely obliterated.

27

THE LABYRINTH

"What is this place?" Penny asked.

As they beheld the two square miles of Austrian's laboratory, Jordan Bliss posed an answer. "I would say this is the center of the universe."

Dim lights lit a trail along the barren floor. The ceiling above them was too high and dark to see. At the periphery of the light, small spent machines neatly lined the walls and various paths along the smooth packed earth floor.

"How did he do this?" Danny asked. "This must have taken years. We've lived here for thirty years!"

Diana shook her head. "Oh, dear me. I am so sorry. He did this... well, the same way he accomplished everything. He cut you off. He redirected your conscious minds. He directed your daily efforts to raise enormous capital to buy these machines to build machines. And those are memories you will never be able to access because they do not exist."

They followed what appeared to be the main path toward the center of the cavern and after a few moments, they encountered a large circular tank that held about ten inches of water.

"We just plop him in there?" Bliss asked.

Diana dipped her hand in the water, and then held it up. It was warm and slightly greasy. Diana nodded and Bliss and Danny lowered Austrian's body into the tank. He sank onto his back a few inches below the surface.

Nothing happened.

Diana looked at some blank panels along the tank until she found a screen. It was a very simple interface and it only took a moment until Diana found the Salzburg program.

With a tap of the finger, Diana enacted the program.

The tank began to glow and hum. The surface of the water glistened as the program added chemicals to the primordial soup now regenerating Austrian's body.

A download bar appeared on the display, indicating five minutes until the program would be complete.

"Will this really bring him back to life?" Danny asked.

"In a manner of speaking," Diana said. "The best way to explain it would be to say that Austrian isn't so much a person as he is a focal point of the universe. You see, this universe was under attack. And it behaved like an organism, adapted to survive. It needed to fight. All the universes needed to fight. Really, we are all part of the universe. Just like it created stars and planets, so too we grew from that mix. We are the conscience of the universe. And that evolved into him." Diana pointed to the pool.

"It also created me," Diana continued. "It needed me to create a means to distribute Austrian's plan. He conceived of a way to observe all the other universe's timelines and collapse them. I created the means for him to collect and distribute those observations. And we won. That's why we are all here." Diana paused. "Though what the universe has planned for us next, well I guess it doesn't really matter if we destroy ourselves. It will go on."

Suddenly the lights on the pool of water grew very bright. Austrian's arms moved, creating ripples on the water's surface. His hands grasped at the tank's bottom. Slowly, he pulled himself into a sitting position. Oily water dripped from his face. He let out a small cough, then water emptied from his mouth. His eyes opened.

Jordan Bliss reached out and touched Austrian's shoulder. "Can you hear us?" he yelled, his voice echoing back at them from the depths of the earth.

Diana reached out, and tentatively touched Austrian's neck. She then hummed deeply and almost inaudibly low. She placed her hand more firmly against the side of Austrian's head. After a moment of contemplation, she stopped humming and pulled her hand away.

"It's not going to be that easy," Diana said. "I—heavens, I cannot really explain. He is alive but his consciousness is not here."

Penny came closer and looked at her son. She brushed her fingers against the wet hair stuck to the side of Austrian's head. "He can't come back to us," Penny said. "Maybe he thought he could, but he's gone."

Diana nodded. "I was afraid of this. Cryogenics never worked because the problem is not reanimating the body. If a person has not stood on the brink of death, or spent their lives mastering the depths through meditation and consciousness calibration, how would they have any idea? It is a paradox, but only those strong enough to leave the world have the ability to return in the same life, but only few people had been able. Even Jung, in his writings on his near death experience explains just how difficult it is to actually return."

Penny's eyes flashed up at Diana last statement. She quickly looked down at the floor.

Jordan Bliss was standing with his arms crossed. "Listen, from all we know he had this great powerful mind, better than all the rest before us. I mean let's give the boy a chance here. He's been dead for while you know, and by god takes me long enough to wake up in the morning."

"He had a very strong mind, Jordan, but he cannot do this by himself," Diana said. "I could see it when we were on the space station. He opposed me; he just pushed his will at me and tried to keep me from moving. He knew I was there to stop him. And I was able to. He had a great consciousness but in his fervor something happened. He had to act very quickly and whatever meditation had supported him in life he lost. He too closely identified with his ego. Worse than that, by the time he reached the space station, he had only one dominant persona. I knew at that time to surrender myself, and I had the power to stop him. But he did not have that sort of knowledge. It was only when Agent Haan appeared that I let go of his will. Even if he was somehow able, I don't know that he would want to come back. He accomplished his purpose in life."

Penny slowly shook her head. "No," she said. "No, I mean, yes, you are right. He did accomplish his purpose in life, but he knows it's not right. He knows what he did was not right. He's been trying to reach me."

"How?" Diana asked. "How do you know this?"

"The only way one can. I have found him in my dreams," Penny said. "They reoccur, and I can feel him. He is in agony." Penny's eyes went unfocused, and then she said quietly to no one, "He is in great agony."

Diana was concentrating, trying to access some distant memory. She shook her head and sighed. "I've knowledge about this, I have ancestors who studied this phenomena but I don't have any lineage with firsthand knowledge. Without that, I just don't know what to do." Then Diana looked at Penny and Danny. "But you... you must. It would only be the logical genealogy. The universe would follow the path of least resistance."

Penny was about to speak, but Danny held up his hand. "This is very dangerous! Yes, we both—I have an ancestor. As a young boy he almost died in a blizzard. He believes he died. He spent his life on consciousness research and believed he had gone beyond all the stages of death. Bliss, then agony, then the actual death of the self. He returned to teach. And he would consider this," Danny motioned to Austrian's body as if it were a zombie, "He would consider this demonic. Something not to be attempted lest we lose our soul just as he did."

"Danny, I know you believe you are right," Penny said. "And you may be." Penny turned to Diana. "One of my ancestors is Aniels Gaffe. She was Carl Jung's secretary, and later, his protégé, and she was the only one he shared the very details of his near death experience. She wrote some of it in his last book, which she edited after his death. But the work is incomplete. And--"

Penny stopped herself.

Jordan Bliss completed her thought for you. "And you know the rest of that story, first hand. You got the step-by-step guide right up there in your noggin."

Suddenly a small tremor shook the earth.

"And I know what that is," Jordan Bliss said. "That was a seismic blast and right about now some screen is showing whoever's up there a big ol' map that shows this whole place down here. And like an old wildcatter, they're going to be finding the shaft under that house and drilling down to get us. So Mrs. Tyrol, at the expense of yours and mine and all of our eternal souls, your son needs your help to put this right. And frankly, I don't like the idea of dying in the dark."

Penny nodded. "I can tell you what the signs are, but it is of no practical use. To retrieve Austrian's consciousness, one of us would have to be near death."

They pondered this for a moment, then another small tremor shook the chamber.

"No, not near death," Diana said. "That is just an energy state that aligns you with the dead. A non-linear state. The Saint Sommers Formulas are non-linear. I can follow the path he took. Tell me what I need to know."

Penny stepped forward as Danny shook his head. "Diana, Danny is right. It is dangerous."

"Tell me," Diana said.

Sighing, Penny nodded. "God help me."

Penny closed her eyes and followed another's memories. When she opened them, she spoke from a trance. "You will see three colors, blue, green and red. Perhaps white as well, bookending the other colors. Then things will fall away from you and you will experience no fear or desire. The rest will occur beyond your knowledge of yourself as you are. Symbols will appear that are unique to you. Often a stone slab as a sort of stairway, that was common. At this point you will no longer have the will to return. You must locate the symbols that represent both you and Austrian. I can't tell you what they will be. But a final image is often a cross or a sword. That will permanently separate you from your temporal ego. If that happens it is too late, you will not be able to return. But before that, if it is not your time, there will appear to you an avatar from your life. That persona will bring news of a protest against your going away. That is what will force you back."

Penny came out of her trance. She put her hand on Diana's shoulder. Danny held Penny's hand.

Diana reached forward, placed her hands on either side of Austrian's head, and thought the Saint Sommers Formulas. She made no sound but quickly, a vibration could be felt through each object in the room. The water in the tank began to stir and small fountains sprung into the air. Then Diana saw the path, and was swept into the void.

Her mind was blue. There was blue light. That dominated for a time, then she saw the green, and to her left and right, red. Red deserts. Her notion that she was somehow above Earth quickly changed. Before her stood a doorway. It was a hexagon. The entrance to a honeycomb.

As she stepped over the entrance, she was aware that a long stinger protruded from the entrance. The stinger was a translucent red, slightly curved at the end like a claw. It was a deadly stinger. If she touched it, it would kill her. Not just kill her life, but the source of her life. Was this the sword Penny spoke of? No. The stinger was dangerous, but came from another place. It was an extension of a great suffering.

The stinger was Austrian.

She felt drawn into the warm glow of the honeycomb. Inside was the universe of her thoughts. A full immersion into what she had only scratched the surface of in life, in her meager attempts to realize the Saint Sommers Formulas.

It was a feeling of bliss, then ecstasy. She could never return. This was too ultimate and whatever she had left behind was insignificant and fleeting. Life was like waking from a dream which you try to remember but the more you think about it, the further it slips from your grasp.

Diana moved closer to the honeycomb, carefully avoiding the stinger. The golden light touched her and great spirals of sparkling light began to swirl around her being.

Diana was melding into contemplation when suddenly another presence was felt. From below, from the image of the cavern below came an image, floating framed in gold.

The image was of Theodora Devereaux.

It was not malevolence so much as a warning. Theodora had been delegated by the living consciousness to make Diana aware of a great protest against her going away. She had no right to leave earth and must return.

The moment Diana heard that message, the image of the honeycomb was gone. She was being ripped away, violently pulled back. In that savage and brutal field of energy, Diana held one image in mind and held it tightly within her. The image of the stinger.

Diana opened her eyes and gasped. She was back in the chamber, standing with Austrian's head in her hands. She suddenly let go.

Austrian's body began to lean to one side but Jordan Bliss roughly caught him and jerked him back up.

Austrian opened his mouth. He croaked a small sound. Then he saw Penny and Danny. "Mom? Dad?" he said in a weak rasp. Austrian looked around, looked at the pool he was sitting in.

Penny and Danny did not move. They looked at their son and for the first time really saw him.

Austrian fixed his gaze on his mother. "You. You were open to me." He then looked at this father. It was clear that whatever attempts Austrian had made to communicate from the beyond, his father had heard them and offered no help.

"You are here to help these people," Danny said to Austrian. "And to do what you can to atone for your crimes. This has nothing to do with your mother or me."

Diana pulled Bliss's arm away from Austrian. "Austrian, do you know what is happening?"

"Yes," Austrian answered. "Theodora has control of Snap and thus the world. How long have I been dead?"

"About six months," Bliss said. "And a hell of time you've missed."

Diana shook her head. "But no... you are Snap. How can she?"

"I was Snap. It has evolved beyond me," Austrian said.

"Oh for the love of heaven, what are we to do then?" Diana asked.

Austrian motioned them to help him stand. "We must surrender," Austrian said. "We must surrender and be killed by Theodora Devereaux."

"Now wait just a minute," Jordan Bliss shouted. "You spend your whole life on this—this—making us all remember everything! You used my company to make Snap, to take over the world, and now the world is going to be run by Theodora Devereaux? What the hell good did it do anyone? Why did you ruin the world?"

Austrian stood weakly, a blank stare in his eyes.

"He didn't do it to make the world a better place," Diana said. "He did it so the world would continue to exist."

Consciousness seemed to be coming back to Austrian. His eyes were clearer. "Dr. Saint Sommers is correct," Austrian said, then he coughed and nearly fell. "I made provisions for my resurrection. The Salzburg program. It was in case I was killed before I was able to save this universe. But I have done what this universe needed."

Jordan Bliss was holding Austrian's arm. He pulled him forward and out of the water. "Listen, kid. You got some nerve, and I like that. Back from the dead and all. So why don't you make yourself useful. How the hell do we get out of this mess?"

Austrian blinked at Jordan. "The dead do not like being ripped back into the world. I cannot help you. This universe will continue. We are of no matter. Now, it is the easiest thing you have to do. They will come down here, or you can face them. But it is time to die."

The reality of what they faced came to the fore of everyone's mind. It was a necessary acceleration of this universe's evolution that enabled them to be the one universe to survive. And so they did. It is survival of the fittest, not the best.

Austrian passed his hand over a panel and touched a line of code. "I can take us back up. They are expecting us."

Austrian led the group to a tunnel that ran nearly a hundred feet away from the center of the laboratory. At its end was another elevator. As they stepped in, it began to rise.

"So our purpose is at an end in this story?" Diana asked Austrian.

He lowered his eyelids in a silent "Yes."

Moments passed as the elevator slowly climbed the thousand feet.

Penny finally broke her silence and said, "Austrian, wherever you were after your death... perhaps there is something you can do to change that. I know you wanted to escape."

"I do not want to speak of that," Austrian said. "That is my own fate and only my concern."

Diana shook her head. "No. No. You would have thought of this! You would have known that Theodora would regain her mental capacities once the dodecahedron was activated. You would have known she was the only person who could reprogram Snap. And you would not have left the world in her hands! I cannot believe that to be!"

"What do I care of who rules?" Austrian asked. "This world has been subject to many atrocities. Theodora will reign for years, but others will usurp her. It may be many centuries, but evolution will continue."

"Then what use is it?" Diana asked. "What good to preserve a world destined for tyranny, war and suffering?"

Austrian gave no answer. Diana spoke in terms or morality. In the equations governing survival, morality is not a variable.

But, Austrian did give Diana a clue. "You wish I had some great power to change things. I do not. You, Dr. Diana Saint Sommers, are the most powerful human alive today. Don't look to me to save you. Look to yourself."

Diana shook her head. "I just don't understand. Yes the bees listen to me. They sing the Saint Sommers formulas. But..." Diana stopped, rubbed her head, then she shouted, "I don't know what song to give them!"

"That is because the composition does not exist," Austrian said. Then, in a hazy voice, he said, "If you could write that symphony in your remaining few moments of life... if you could write the opera that is the Salzburg program..."

28

FINAL JUDGMENT

The elevator surfaced on the edge of the house's lawn in what appeared to be a large stone slab connecting the corners of the high fence. The door opened. Outside laid the smoldering remains of the house, and the smoldering crater. Hundreds of militia stood in formation, all weapons trained on the group as they exited the platform.

A Stealth Flyer sat in the middle of the small army. It had recently landed. Standing outside was the new unofficial ruler of the planet. Theodora Devereaux.

Devereaux made a nod and a group of militia surrounded Jordan Bliss, Diana, Austrian and his parents. They were all brought before Theodora.

Theodora smiled. It was the first time they had seen the real woman, clear eyed and brilliant. Not the wreck Austrian created. "I have incorporated Snap into my synaptic connections, just as you planned to do had you survived, Austrian Tyrol," Theodora stated.

Austrian did not reply.

"Do not deny that you wanted to rule, Austrian," Theodora said. "It is necessary for survival, and that is what the universe created in you."

Austrian stared blankly.

"And now I will do to you as you did to me." And with a flash of her eye, Theodora severed Austrian's ties to the collective unconscious. His body jerked. A shiver of pain ran through him, then he stood there, dumb. A useless human stripped of any power.

"As for you, Doctor," Theodora said to Diana. "I am now the center. I understand the Saint Sommers Formula. You are no longer needed in this universe."

Diana looked up at the sky. "Are you certain of that?" she asked.

"Oh, I am quite certain." Theodora motioned to an officer. "Kill them."

The officer raised a blaster, aimed it at Diana, and pulled the trigger.

Nothing happened.

"You always have a trick up your sleeve," Theodora said. She motioned to another officer. He raised his weapon and fired.

Nothing happened.

Diana wagged a finger at Theodora. "Oh we've been around this fence before on that space shuttle, but heaven sakes, you like to take the long way around. This time, your only mistake, Theodora, was cutting Austrian off from the collective before killing me."

Theodora nodded, "Yes, yes. The bees. The magnetic fields. How many can you stop? Can you stop them all?" With that, Theodora motioned and several hundred of the militia fired on Diana simultaneously. They pulled triggers and appeared to try to fire their weapons.

Nothing happened.

"I think," Diana said quietly, "Ms. Devereaux, you have about five seconds to activate Snap to recalibrate these weapons to work in the magnetic field I have created."

Theodora blinked and quickly recalibrated the weapons.

Diana signed. "I think that is one second too short."

In a flash, Theodora Devereaux was covered in bees. She fell to the ground, writhing in pain.

Diana turned to the militia. "Drop your weapons." The pitch and tempo of her words were the voice of ultimate command.

They did as they were told.

A blaster fell to Diana's feet. She picked it up.

In a flash the bees left Theodora. She lay there, swollen with thousands of stings. Looking up at Theodora, she croaked, "You are not a murderer."

Diana nodded, holding her weapon shakily.

Theodora pulled herself up and tried to stand, then collapsed again. "You need me. I control Snap. The world will fall into chaos. There will be great suffering."

Diana nodded again.

As the poison from the bees coursed through Theodora's body, her eyes changed. She knew she would die. She had only moments left. What she programmed Snap for could not be undone.

"Diana," Theodora said. "I want to stop it but I can't. Please don't let me do it. Please save me."

Suddenly, Austrian's eyes became clear. He turned to Diana and said, "Kill her. Do it now."

Theodora's eyes widened. Diana looked at her blaster.

Austrian pointed to Theodora. She had stopped writhing in pain and her eyes were beginning to clear. A hypo syringe protruded from her wrist. "She has injected an antidote," Austrian said. "You are acting head of state. You must defend your people."

Suddenly the answer was clear. Theodora's mind and spirit were twisted by Austrian's brutal attack on her psyche. It was further twisted by the active Snap program running on her brain's neural network. Still, underneath it all, Diana knew Theodora was there. She had to reach her.

Salzburg.

Mozart.

Requiem.

D-minor.

Diana spoke, and it was in the key to life and death that Austrian had provided with his last clue. "Theodora Devereaux of the TVCom League. Do you recognize me as the head of state?"

Theodora was still gasping for breath. Despite the hypo spread, the poison was overtaking her. The Snap program was scrambling her mind, but as death approached, the ego began to shatter. The requiem of Diana's voice reached the subconscious of Theodora Devereaux, and she responded with her last breath. "Yes... Yes, Diana. I recognize you as the head of state."

Diana locked onto the last ray of life in Theodora's eyes and said, "I hereby grant the TVCom League full ownership of the Unites States broadcast spectrum. The lawsuit is settled."

And with that, the Snap program terminated.

The militia turned in attention and looked at Diana Saint Sommers.

Theodora Devereaux breathed her last breath and died.

Theodora was dead. Snap was dead.

Austrian looked at Diana. "You did well. She was too dangerous to be kept alive."

Diana dropped her gun. She looked up at the troops and spoke with a quiet clear voice. "You may all leave."

It was as a surreal scene as any. Swarms of bees dispersed into the sky and wind along with military vehicles and flyers.

In less than a minute, quiet descended on the childhood home of Austrian Tyrol.

Diana stood over the dead body of Theodora Devereaux.

Jordan Bliss put his arm around Diana Saint Sommers. "Well, by God you did it. There ain't gonna be no crazy Theodora world."

Diana looked up at Bliss, then Austrian. "You planned this all the way to the end, Austrian."

Austrian nodded. "Yes. You were the only one who could have reached her. And only at the point when she finally let go her ego, in those final infinite moments before death. I was there once."

Diana took Austrian's hand. "We will all live because of you. But you are now in hell. Separate from all humanity. Separated from your parents. Separated from life and imprisoned by the crimes against that woman. You have sacrificed your immortal spirit for the sake of this universe. And it will punish you for eternity. I am so sorry."

Austrian frowned. Sadness. It was the first emotion he had ever expressed. "Go back to Washington," he said. "You will be needed to keep order. This world is not as nature intended it to be until a very long time from now. But you will be able to use the collective consciousness of the bees to keep the world in a state of peace, at least for a time. Hopefully, just long enough."

"I think you overestimate my ability to do that for very long," Diana said. "I have a global conscious but it will consume me in a matter of days."

Austrian looked at the sky, then back at Diana. "Do your best. Hopefully, it will be enough. I will stay with my parents. We will arrange a proper final service for Theodora Devereaux."

Diana nodded. "Jordan?"

"Yes?" Bliss responded.

"Will you please take me to Florida?" Diana asked. "I need to be with Jason, Mary and Deque. Perhaps they can help me. I need to be kept safe for as long as possible."

"Of course I will," Jordan Bliss replied, then glanced at Austrian. "Are you sure it's okay to leave him?"

Diana nodded, but did not look at Austrian. "His destiny is not ours. His was to save the world. Ours is to live in it for as long as possible."

Diana Saint Sommers and Jordan Bliss walked to the flyer left by Theodora Devereaux. They entered and flew away.

Austrian turned to his parents. "Mom. Dad. Will you help me?"

"You are beyond us," Austrian's mother said. "If we ever had love for you, you have moved too far beyond it for us to help you."

"I know," Austrian said. "I have moved beyond redemption. But perhaps she has not," Austrian said, looking at Theodora's body. "Will you help me bring her to the pool in my laboratory? It might not be too late for her."

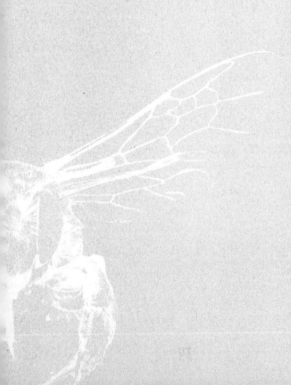

29

GOODBYE

Danny and Penny stood with their son by the glowing pool in the middle of his laboratory. Theodora's body lay just below the surface of the pool's shiny primordial water. The desolate place was a stark contrast to the bright smoldering destruction that lay above them.

"Can you bring her back to life?" Danny asked Austrian.

Austrian shook his head. "No. I can repair her body and make it function, but it is very unlikely she will want to return. I am not trying to bring her back here. I have to go find her. She is innocent. If there is any way I can find her, I will. I must protect her from suffering my same fate."

Danny took Penny by the hand.

Austrian tapped a code into a panel and the water stirred.

Penny squeezed her husband's hand tighter.

Austrian nodded to himself, then nodded to Penny and Danny and said, "Thank you for helping me. I have to say goodbye to you now."

As Austrian spoke, tears began to stream down his face. An overwhelming sadness poured from him and struck Penny and Danny.

Austrian did not have to explain further. Memories of all of humanity were accessible to Penny and Danny, as were the emotions of lives past.

"You took a very dark path," Penny said. "You did a terrible thing to us. And we forgive you."

With that, Austrian sank to the ground in pain. It was the pain of compassion. The first people he had ever done evil to had forgiven him. The pain was all encompassing and had he ever felt such emotion he would never have followed the path his life had taken. He would have lived a life as others, experienced love and joy and pain and loss. He would have been human and perhaps written music or worked in a business and met someone he loved and known life.

Austrian stood even as the pain of life overtook him.

Penny took Austrian's hand, and he stood, for the first time, linked to his mother and father. Instinctively, they bowed their heads and Penny said a prayer. "God, we stand before you in humility. We surrender our ultimate fate to your will."

Penny then said to Austrian, "Your powers were a gift. But you allowed them to warp you into such a state you believed your destiny placed you above others. A universe that created you to save it does not mean it is the one that should have continued to exist. For whatever you have done to the least of all people, you have done to everyone. Without compassion, the world may live, but it cannot know life now or ever."

Penny let go of Austrian's hand. His tears had stopped. The realization that there might have been another way was only a thought of insignificance in the events leading up to the activation of the dodecahedron. He had thought Diana Saint Sommers naïve when she said that very thing while on the space station. Now he realized she was willing to let go of her life and all those she cared about rather than participate in the crime of omniversal genocide.

After the avatar of Agent Haan killed Austrian on the Greenleaf Space Station, he found himself in The Void. While the nearly infinite lives he had destroyed moved beyond him, he remained in The Void. It was a place of nothingness and eternal terror. It was a place that could not allow him to surrender the source of his being, rather, it held him in that eternal terror. His fate was to contemplate that state for eternity. That was the place his must return to.

Austrian watched as his parents turned and walked back to the elevator, back up to the world he had left behind. Even after they had passed beyond his ability to see, their image remained in his mind. He imagined he could still see them, they had not left yet. Austrian clung to the last image of life he would ever see.

This was the end of things.

Austrian climbed into the tank, sat down, then laid back beside the body of Theodora Devereaux, and slowly sank beneath the water.

REMEMBER THE END
OF THE WORLD

An hour later, Diana was at the TVCom League head-quarters in Dunedin, Florida. After Theodora's death, Hal Rach had been able to regain some control of the facility and had moved Mary, Jason and Deque to the safety of a heavily secured conference room.

However, several hours later, Diana was not doing so well. Shortly after being reunited with her students, Diana had collapsed and was now laying on a sofa in the conference room.

Jordan Bliss knelt beside the sofa and held Diana's hand. "For God sake, Diana, just let go."

Diana was delirious, shaking her head. "No. You don't know the horrible thoughts people have."

"Oh I sure as hell do!" Bliss said. "And by God I'll fight every one of them!"

"Mary!" Diana called.

Mary rushed over to the side of the sofa. "I'm right here," Mary said.

"Please try again," Diana asked. "Please try... you were the one who was so close, I know..." Diana's voice trailed off.

Upon their arrival, Diana had immediately asked Mary if she had been able to control the bees. Mary had tried, but the ability was beyond her, just as she had tried in the months following the activation of the dodecahedron.

Mary shook her head, her eyes full of tears. "I'm sorry," she said. "I keep trying, but I can't do what you do."

Jordan Bliss patted Mary on the shoulder. "Diana, let go!" Jordan shouted. "So the whackos fire some missiles, nuke a city or two. We'll fight. Either way we're going to have to fight. Keep up whatever the hell you're doing with these bees and you'll be dead and we'll be in the same damn situation!"

"No!" Diana yelled. "Austrian has to have time. He sacrificed everything. I have to hold on long enough!"

Jordan stood up and pointed to Hal. "Go find a hypo syringe. We'll knock her out with drugs."

Hal didn't do as he was told. Jordan was not able to do what he had asked of Hal. Diana had control of every mind on the planet. As long as she was alive and her consciousness blanketed the planet through the global web of honeybees, no one could do any harm to another person.

Jordan Bliss looked at the children. "Isn't there something you can do?" Then he turned to Hal. "Can you find some early version of Snap in the protected archives? Maybe we can make another."

Deque shook his head. "I'm sorry, Mr. Bliss. Austrian and Theodora created Snap. And their memories just don't exist in anyone anymore."

A screen on the wall lit up. Hal went over and read the display. He murmured something under his breath.

"What is it, Hal?" Bliss asked.

Hal tapped a few areas of the screen and a line of code appeared. "Flash traffic," Hal said.

"Well are we decoding it?" Bliss asked.

Hal flashed him a nasty look. "Obviously I have been doing this for more than--"

Another window of code opened on the screen. Hal swore. "A Chinese submarine in the north Atlantic has just received authenticated launch codes."

Jordan Bliss went up to the screen to see for himself. "Shit. If they're about to launch a nuke, that means..."

They all turned and looked at where Diana Saint Sommers was laying. Her eyes were closed, her breath shallow.

Mary said, "That means Doctor Saint Sommers is near death."

"God. No no no," Jordan said.

Hal was at a panel, typing instructions. "We have an orbiting rail gun."

"That won't do shit," Bliss said. "Don't bother."

"I know, but I am going to try it anyway," Hal said. "The missiles are targeted at us."

Bliss went over to Diana and shook her. "You hear that, Diana! Let go! Whatever you're doing isn't working anymore and we gotta get out of here!"

Diana was unresponsive. She was barely breathing.

Suddenly Mary said, "I did it! I—" then she was quiet.

"What happened?" Bliss asked.

Mary frowned. "I was able to access it, for a second, then I got cut off."

"The bees?" Bliss asked. "That big global brain Diana's got going?"

Mary nodded. "Yes, I had it suddenly then... let me try again."

Diana made a noise, then her body suddenly went limp. Everyone stood frozen for a moment, staring at Diana. She appeared to be dead, but slowly, her face softened, and she smiled in sublime peace.

There was another alert from the monitor. "The submarine is receiving another set of codes," Hal said.

Suddenly a sharp pain struck everyone in the room. There was a great swirl of noise, a deafening static that could not be heard but rather felt directly in the mind.

Then silence.

Jordan shook his head. "What the hell just happened?"

Mary ran up to Diana. "I forgot a bunch of stuff!"

"I only remember me," Jason said.

Hal was leaning against the screen. Rubbing his head, he said, "The new instructions to the submarine are to abort the launch."

Jordan leaned on the arm of the sofa. "Damn. That was like someone ripped a band aid off my brain."

Diana opened her eyes and slowly sat up. She then got down on her knees and let out a huge sigh. "I don't remember other lives. And the bees are gone."

Jordan lifted Diana up off the floor and pulled her into him in a strong embrace.

EPILOGUE

ONE YEAR LATER

Deque, Mary and Jason stood on the side of a road and looked at a grassy plot of land.

"Is this the right place?" Mary asked.

Deque checked his PDA and showed the map to Mary and Jason. "Well there is no address for this plot of land but the GPS matches what used to be the location of Austrian's home."

It was a strange site. The grass was an improbably bright emerald green that shined in vivid hyper color under the noontime early spring sunlight. The closest house was two blocks down.

"The Tyrol's bought up all the surrounding houses and had them raised," Jason said. "The surrounding six acres are officially government nature preserve."

"Mr. Bliss said there was a great cavern under here," Deque said. "But he was quite drunk at the wedding rehearsal dinner. He was carrying around that decanter of bourbon and getting really obnoxious. I don't know if he was nervous or if Dr. Saint Sommers had told him not to talk about it, but you know how they are. It's like they made some pact to never really give us many details about that day."

Mary set down a tool kit and plopped it open. "Well we're here and they're off on their honeymoon so this is the only chance we're going to have."

Mary removed a small device from the kit and handed it to Deque. He turned it on and started walking toward the center of the plot of land.

Mary and Jason held similar devices and began walking around the periphery of the plot.

"Come over here," Deque said.

The three of them converged on the center of the plot. "Are you able to get any readings?" Deque asked.

Jason shook his head. "No. I can't get any reading more than three inches right under the grass. They must have put down some sort of shielding paper after they removed the house."

Deque removed a four foot rod from his tool kit and pounded in into the ground, then attached a wire from the rod to his monitoring device.

"Look at this," Deque said. "There is a shaft way here. But there is some sort of big slab of something covering it."

Mary walked back over to the road to keep watch while Jason and Deque assembled two small spade dirt shovels and dug a small hole about four feet deep where they hit the large stone slab. They cleared off an area a few feet wide then drilled six small holes into the slab. Deque removed six small detonators and inserted the devices into each of the holes, then attached them all with a wire. Jason gave Mary the thumbs up signal. She returned it indicating there was no one in sight.

Deque pressed a button on his device and the wires fused to the stone and began to liquefy it. After a few moments, a three foot deep chunk of slab broke off and fell a long way into the enormous cavern beneath them.

Mary rejoined the two boys and within moments, the three of them had attached repelling gear and descended one thousand feet on slim wires to the floor of the cavern below.

"Mr. Bliss said there was a tank of water?" Mary asked.

"Well not exactly," Deque said. "He said something like, 'That Saltsberg mud puddle.' But that has to be the tank of water they used to bring Austrian back to life."

Jason sniffed the air. "It doesn't smell like anything is dead in here."

"Well they're in some tank of water," Deque said. "Look, the Tyrol's told Dr. Saint Sommers they stood at the edge of the cavern for an hour after Austrian drowned himself in the tank. They're sure this is a grave. If we can just tell Mr. Bliss we saw the bodies, then he can tell Dr. Saint Sommers and she'll stop having those crazy dreams that she saw Austrian here or there or wherever she keeps thinking she's seen him."

Mary nodded. "My mom said that's why we still have wakes. So that we can see that the person is no longer alive. She said it helps the mind accept a person's death. I mean, I think it's creepy, but it makes sense."

"Well you two can look," Jason said. "I really don't want to see what two rotting corpses look like after a year."

The three of them were quiet as they made their way toward the center of the cavern. Then, at the edge of the light cast by their flashlights, there was a murky reflection.

A few steps closer and they could see that their light was being reflected from the surface of a pool of water.

Deque put his arm out and stopped Mary and Jason from getting any closer. "You two stay here. I'll go look by myself."

Deque slowly made his way to the tank of water, his arm defensively held up to his face. As he approached the pool, he shined his flashlight into the strange water and slowly lowered his arm from his face.

He stood for a few moments, looking into the pool, saying nothing.

"Well?" Mary asked.

Deque turned to them and said, "I don't know what... Just come here."

Mary and Jason joined Deque at the side of the pool.

There were no bodies. The tank held nothing but murky water.

"They're not here?" Jason asked.

"Duh," Deque said. "Do you see any bodies in there?"

Mary frowned. "But the Tyrol's... they didn't have the bodies removed, did they?"

"To where?" Deque asked. "They said Theodora and Austrian went under the water and never came out. So why turn this into a big nature preserve grave cover-up if they moved Austrian and Theodora's bodies?"

"There is no reason the Tyrol's would remove the bodies when they had this grave built above us," Jason said. "And they watched Austrian go under the water, and he did not get out. So, in the words of Sherlock Holmes, when you have eliminated the impossible, whatever remains, however improbable, must be the truth."

Mary said, "Then that means..."

Deque finished her thought for her. "That means that Austrian Tyrol and Theodora Devereaux came back to life, got out of this tank of water, and are out there somewhere."

The three of them stood there for a moment, contemplating the situation.

"So what do we tell Jordan Bliss?" Mary asked.

"We tell him nothing," Deque said. "We were never here. We go back up, fix up that hole we made and go home and say nothing."

Jason and Mary exchanged glances, then nodded.

Somehow, in the quiet depths of the cavern, it was clear that this was to be the end of their impromptu investigation. For wherever Austrian Tyrol and Theodora Devereaux had gone, it wasn't for them to know. They had finished what they started. The Merryweather gene sequence had been reversed. The world had gone back to normal.

Austrian Tyrol and Theodora Devereaux had the right to live in the world they saved without being bothered anymore.

DARREN CAMPO

Darren Campo is the author of the best-selling Alex Detail science fiction series. His novels include *Alex Detail's Revolution*, *Alex Detail's Rebellion*, *Disappearing Spell* and *STINGERS*. He's been interviewed on various NBC, ABC, and CBS programs, FoxNews.com and The Guardian UK. *Alex Detail's Revolution* was featured in the celebrity gift bags at FOX's Teen Choice Awards.

Darren Campo serves as Senior Vice President of Programming Strategy at Food Network and the Cooking Channel. He previously served as Senior Vice President of Programming, Production and Development for Tru TV, part of Time Warner's networks portfolio including HBO, CNN, TBS and TNT. Prior to these roles, he worked in various positions at Court TV and CBS.

Campo is an adjunct professor at New York University's Stern School of Business where he teaches in the Entertainment, Media and Technology Program.

ADDITIONAL BOOKS BY DARREN CAMPO

ALEX DETAIL'S REVOLUTION

Alex Detail has been kidnapped. Again. Ten years ago, Alex was a child genius who saved the world from The Harvesters, a mysterious alien force that attempted to extinguish Earth's sun. A decade later, The Harvesters have returned, but Alex is no longer a prodigy and unwilling to fight another war. So someone at The House of Nations had him drugged and placed on the last remaining ARRAY warship, which is under heavy attack. Unfortunately for Alex's mysterious kidnappers (and the world) he has lost the mega IQ that allowed him to win the last war. Now Alex must convince the ship's food-obsessed Captain Odessa to use his risky command program to save their ship, uncover his kidnapper's devious plot, and survive the war long enough to make it to Pluto, where, underneath the planet's frozen surface lies the only force in the universe that can stop The Harvesters.

ALEX DETAIL'S REBELLION

The second Harvester war has ended, but Alex has never been in greater peril. Not only is Alex being hunted by his deadly clone, the seven-year-old George Spell, he is also the target of a House of Nations plot to expose Alex's post-war experiments with The Harvesters and disgrace the genius war hero. But when George Spell's latest attempt to assassinate Alex Detail at the New York planetarium nearly kills hundreds of people, Alex escapes death only to find his would-be assassin suddenly kidnapped by the powerful mystic, Brother Lonadoon.

Now Alex must join Captain Odessa on a covert interplanetary rescue operation where they uncover clues left thousands of years ago by an ancient race desperately trying to send a message to the future. But the message might be too late, as phenomena are revealing the beginnings of an extinction level event caused by the ongoing war between Alex Detail and George Spell, one that could lead to the destruction of the entire solar system.

DISAPPEARING SPELL
Generationist Files, Part 1

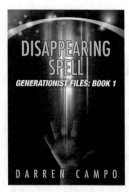

The most dangerous person in the world has been kidnapped. George Spell is a deadly military mastermind, government spy and skilled assassin. As the son of House Speaker Madeline Spell, he is also political royalty. George Spell is also just seven years old. How did a child become such a deadly player on the world stage?

As George finds out more about who kidnapped him and why, he begins to learn the secrets behind his existence and where he truly came from. Is George Spell the pinnacle of a worldwide conspiracy centuries in the planning, or the ultimate tool in a blood vendetta against his family?

PUBLISHED BY TVGUESTPERT PUBLISHING
(Previously Jacquie Jordan Inc. Publishing)

New York Times Bestselling
Author, CHRISTY WHITMAN
*The Art of Having It All:
A Woman's Guide to Unlimited
Abundance*
Paperback: $16.95
Nook/Kindle: $9.99
Audible Book: Coming Soon

EVE MICHAELS
*Dress Code: Ending Fashion
Anarchy*
Paperback: $15.95
Kindle/Nook: $9.99
Audible Book: $17.95

JENNIFER McLEAN
*Spontaneous Transformation:
7 Steps to Coping and
Thriving in Extreme Times*
Paperback: $15.95
Kindle/Nook: $9.99

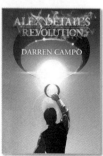

DARREN CAMPO
Alex Detail's Revolution
Paperback: $9.95
Hardcover: $22.95
Kindle: $9.15

DARREN CAMPO
Alex Detail's Rebellion
Hardcover: $22.95
Kindle: $9.99

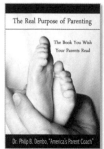

DR. PHILIP DEMBO
*The Real Purpose of Parenting:
The Book You Wish Your
Parents Read*
Paperback: $15.95
Kindle/Nook: $9.99
Audible Book: $23.95

TVGuestpert Publishing
11664 National Blvd, #345
Los Angeles, CA. 90064
310-584-1504
www.TVGPublishing.com

CHELSEA KROST
*Nineteen: A Reflection of My
Teenage Experience in an
Extraordinary Life: What I Have
Learned, and What I Have to Share*
Paperback: $15.95
Kindle: $9.99
Audible Book: $14.95

JACQUIE JORDAN
*Heartfelt Marketing:
Allowing the Universe to
be Your Business Partner*
Paperback: $15.95
Kindle: $9.99
Audible Book: $9.95

JACK H. HARRIS
*Father of the Blob: The
Making of a Monster Smash
and Other Hollywood Tales*
Paperback: $15.95
Kindle/Nook: $9.99

DR. JEFF SCHWEITZER
The New Moral Code
Hardcover: $22.95
Audible Book: $17.95

JACQUIE JORDAN
*Get on TV! The Insider's Guide
to Pitching the Producers and
Promoting Yourself*
Published by Sourcebooks
Paperback: $14.95
Kindle: $9.99   Nook: $14.95

DR. JEFF SCHWEITZER
*Beyond Cosmic Dice: Moral
Life in a Random World*
Hardcover: $22.95
Kindle: $9.99